JUSTIN MORGAN
FOUNDER OF HIS RACE

JUSTIN MORGAN
FOUNDER OF HIS RACE

THE ROMANTIC HISTORY OF A HORSE
ELEANOR WARING BURNHAM

WILDSIDE PRESS

TO

THE MEMORY OF

MY FATHER.

Originally published in 1911.
Published by Wildside Press LLC.
wildsidpress.com

FOREWORD.

The establishment of an historic basis for this little romance was fraught with many difficulties, owing to the great divergence in statement and opinions to be found in regard to the life and origin of JUSTIN MORGAN. The author was obliged to select from a mass of contradictory material that which most nearly conformed with the purpose and continuity of the story.

Therefore, if any find the *history* not to his way of thinking she begs him to realize that it is, after all, but a detail which she hopes may be compensated for by the manner in which she has endeavored to bring out all those noble characteristics for which the FOUNDER OF HIS RACE was famous.

In the frontispiece, modelled by Roger Noble Burnham, the portrait of Mistress Lloyd was posed for by Miss Fifi Willis, of Columbia, Missouri, to whom the author wishes to extend her thanks.

ELEANOR WARING BURNHAM,

(Morgan Horse Club).

MAGNOLIA, MASSACHUSETTS, *September, 1911.*

INTRODUCTION.

The human side of horse-nature may have been touched upon by various writers who have given us glimpses into this realm of thought, but it remained for the author of JUSTIN MORGAN, FOUNDER OF HIS RACE, to introduce us to a real character, as an individual, a horse of tradition, but whose lay is unsung.

Almost forgotten, this horse's *origin was wrapt in obscurity* until recently, yet he became the sire of the most famous breed of horses in America.

Only those who have lived with horses, as I have—out of doors and in my studio—learn to know them as distinct beings, as varied in their make-up and development as the human kind, affected by the same laws and influences that stimulate or smother *our* mental growth.

I dare not tell all I know to be true about the intelligence and sagacity of our horse friends, for fear of having my balance of mind subjected to doubt; but I am quite ready to believe all that this author tells us of equine feelings and faithfulness, for she has been prompted to relate this little tale of OLD JUSTIN MORGAN through love and intimate acquaintance with his descendants.

The author's father was the first to introduce the Morgan horse into the State of Georgia—in 1858—when he purchased the celebrated Enterprise, G.G.G.G. son of JUSTIN MORGAN. Later he took out many others—all of whom made his stock farm, Annandale, famous.

My own inherited associations with Vermont brought me into relation with Morgan horses in childhood, when I listened to tales of their wonderful powers of endurance, strength and intelligence, which maturer years have never made me doubt.

The early Morgan was the best all-round, general-purpose horse ever produced. They were highly valued, and New England breeders—especially the Vermonters—kept the blood pure by breeding in parallel lines and then inbreeding, by which means they established a fixed type that has and will reproduce itself and maintain its characteristics for generations.

For a period of sixty years the Vermonters bred nothing but Morgans, and during the Civil War Vermont was one of the few places where horses could be obtained. They proved so efficient for cavalry purposes that the State was almost stripped of them. It is well known that the best mounted regiments were on Morgan horses.

Their reputation was such that after the war the West Point Academy was furnished with none but Morgans, until about twenty-five years ago the Western horse has been supplied as a substitute, greatly to the detriment of the service.

Following the depletion made in 1861-65 came the popularity of the Hambletonian horse to lead the Vermonters into untried experiments of doubtful value. The result was that, by 1890, the pure Morgan horse was found to be the exception, and the few breeders who realized what had been lost began to cherish the remnants of an almost lost race, and prizes were offered for the best Morgans.

Mr. Joseph Battell, upon whose investigations this author has founded her historic narrative of the first Morgan horse, gathered with infinite pains all the pedigrees he could find and established The Morgan Horse Register, which is now accepted as the authority.

In 1907 the Morgan horse-breeding work of the United States Government received a great impetus when Mr. Battell presented to the Department of Agriculture four hundred acres of fine land lying two miles from Middlebury, Vermont, now known as the Morgan Horse Farm, and equipped with farmhouse, stables, barns, etc., to which were removed all the horses from the Vermont Agricultural Experimental Station, near Burlington.

The Morgan horse has always been noted for his longevity, retaining his spirit and vigor in extreme old age. They are free from almost every species of disease, showing their soundness of constitution. They mature early, and are easily kept, because they are very hardy. To-day they show the traits of OLD JUSTIN MORGAN in their docility and symmetry of form, and this Founder of his race, according to Mr. Battell, was but six generations of English breeding from the original Arab stock, including Byerly Turk and Godolphin Arabian.

The Morgan horse has quietly won all the honors a grateful people can bestow upon him, and we are glad to greet his embodiment of character in this form.

H. K. BUSH-BROWN,

(Morgan Horse Club).

WASHINGTON, D. C.

CHAPTER I.

EARLY INFLUENCES.

Once upon a time—but why should I begin this horse-tale as if it were a mere fairy-tale? It is founded on the story of a real horse in a setting of incidents related in the histories of the various localities in which he lived. Where possible, history has been so closely followed as to use the real names of those vigorous pioneers who helped to make it.

And so, upon a *certain* time—

In 1789,[1] when there were but thirteen stars on the American flag, and George Washington was the newly-made President, near Springfield, Massachusetts, a colt was born, a colt destined to become the founder of the finest breed of horses ever known in America.

A wide, lush pasture on the gently-sloping bottom land, through which the Connecticut River winds its way to the Sound, was the scene of his earliest gambolling.

Poised at a dizzy height, on wobbly, spindly legs, which showed little promise of the symmetry and beauty of later years, he romped near his mother's protecting heels or rested in her shadow.

His merry, laughing companion was a brook which flowed down to the river; he played along its willow-fringed banks, racing with the beckoning waters until out of breath; then, hurrying back to his mother through the gathering dusk, he would return with her to their pleasant stable in the barnyard of Silas Whitman.

His developing colt-nature expanded, day by day, to the beauties and interests about him. He loved the twinkling waters, the overhanging trees, the ferns spiralling among dark-green shadows; the delicate scent of violets, peeping between moss-covered stones, delighted his sensitive nostrils. He loved the birds, fluttering and swaying on boughs and chirping soft, sweet notes. In response to all Nature his small-pointed ears pricked and quivered. He blew his warm breath for fun on butterflies and bees, as they fussed over dew-wet blossoms, but swerved aside, with trembling nostrils, at the strident cry of a jay, waiting in the shadow for *his* chance of a practical joke!

The hoot of an owl, the bark of a fox, the crashing of a squirrel through the branches overhead, would make him scamper to his mother's side, panting and excited.

These were his baby fears; his real and lasting antipathy was to dogs; the distant howling of one seemed to fill him with terror; thunderstorms, too, made him nervous and, so impressible was he to these, he could tell, two days in advance, that one was coming; only much urging could prevail upon him to leave the security of his stable when he felt the approach of one.

Gradually his mother taught him all that one good, faithful horse can teach another, not to show fear, not to shy, not to kick and never to be taken by surprise. He was happy and care-free then, for he did not have to wear hard straps, called harness, nor draw heavy loads, nor wear iron shoes; and his bare, sensitive hoofs soon learned to tell the difference between safe and dangerous ground. His sense of smell was singularly acute and standing close to his mother's side— that she might better brush the flies from both, with her long, useful tail—he learned to distinguish poisonous from wholesome weeds.

Master Whitman called him True Briton, 2d, for his celebrated father, *True Briton*, but the double name was soon shortened to the very appropriate one of "True." And, for convenience, we shall speak of his mother as Gipsey.

Gipsey was one of those mothers, unknown to history, but to whose early influence her son possibly owed much of his success in later life. Sometimes it was necessary for her to reprove him; she nipped him sharply, if he were playful at the wrong time, or kicked too strongly in fun; but she never had to admonish him twice about anything on account of his remarkable memory.

One day, when she had to correct him, and was conscious of having lost her temper, she neighed apologetically.

"Alas, my son, I am no better than a woman!"

This was unjust, as True discovered later, for some of the strongest friendships of his life were for women; he found them ever generous with maple sugar and the goodies for which he quickly learned to whinney at their kitchen windows. They were more appreciative, too, and did not expect him to perform miracles, as men did who set him tasks that taxed every nerve and muscle.

Early each morning Silas Whitman came to the barnyard to play with and train the colt, and from the beginning the little creature showed marvellous characteristics.

Never did True forget his first sight of Man! At that time—being quite new-come into the world—he did not know the ways of different animals, and thought Master Whitman very curious as he walked about on his hind legs! The small colt wondered if he would have to do the same when he grew older and his spindly legs grew stronger. He did not fear the friendly man-creature who played so gently,— little by little training him to obey and afterwards rewarding him with a bit of maple sugar. A kind word and a pat was always given to Gipsey, too, and mother and son very soon began to watch for their master's coming, giving him welcome, with little whinneys, and throaty neighs, when they heard his cheery whistle.

When True's third molar came he had made the acquaintance of a halter. Later in life he came to see that the conveniences of a halter cannot be taught too early. He found out uses for his, all by himself; one was that he could manage to throw the rein over hay that was too high in the rack to reach comfortably, and thus pull it down to an easy height. His mother thought this very ingenious and praised him, which pleased the little fellow very much.

When the first molar of his permanent teeth came he had been taught all about a bridle and bit—things he never liked but made the best of, as Gipsey told him they were inevitable.

When there were errands in the village Silas would hitch Gipsey up to the "shay" and allow True to trot alongside for exercise and experience. He enjoyed these little jaunts under the giant elms that bordered the street, carpeted with a patchwork of sifting sunshine and cool shadow.

Over garden fences he could see green, succulent box-hedges and one day, when he found a gate open, he trotted boldly in to get a taste!

Scarcely had he begun to nibble when a dog dashed round the corner of the house, a boy at his heels. When the latter caught sight of the intruder he gave a whoop and urged the dog to nip at True's feet. The colt, startled, made a quick movement of self-protection with his hard little heels and struck the dog on the head, effectually silencing his bark and rolling him over in the dirt.

A rock hit the colt's side, but he did not tarry; excitedly, he plunged out of the open gate and raced down the road after his mother, now full half mile away. The odor of box was ever after associated, disagreeably, with boys and dogs in his mind.

When he related the incident to his friend, Caesar, the yellow stable cat, the latter purred conviction and confided that for untold generations dogs had been the sworn enemies of his family.

"It *may* be possible for a boy, occasionally, to be polite and gentle; I do not know," mewed the cat. "But as for dogs! Well, you must unsheath your claws and arch your back on sight!"

Caesar was an independent cat of wide experience and had travelled and lived in many barns; his opinion, therefore, had weight with True. One day, whilst rubbing against the colt's leg, in his affectionate way, he remarked that if it had not been for Gipsey and True he would long since have returned to his last barn-home, where the mice had a sweeter flavor on account of a careless housewife who often left her cheese-box open.

"Besides," he added, strutting about and waving his tail with careless dignity, "there is a very nice tortoiseshell pussy waiting there for me!"

"But, do you know the way back?" asked True, interested and not failing to admire, and be duly impressed, by Caesar's swagger and importance.

"I know the way back well enough," the cat bragged; but added with disgust, "In very truth, the jade who put me in the bag forgot to shake the dust out of it; but such a trifle could not blind *me*!"

A very happy playground was the Whitman barnyard. Beside the horses there were two little red-and-white calves who romped in a way that entertained but almost drove Caesar crazy. Before them he would flee, round and round, instead of getting out of their way at once!

A curly-tailed, twinkling-eyed pig, very fat and funny, shared their life for a time; but one day he disappeared, noisily, and never returned.

In those days the memory of the British was fresh in the minds of all; the War of the Revolution had been over but a short eight years and the name "Red-Coat" still had an ominous sound. Gipsey, being an American mother, taught her son to hate the British and told him war-tales that made him quiver with patriotism.

One day the colt invented a game which he called "Chasing the Red-Coat," and fine fun it was, to be sure! With one accord the calves and True made Caesar the "Red-Coat" because he was such a fleet runner! That Caesar did not think much of the game was obvious as he dashed wildly at a tree and running up its trunk sat spluttering at them, his fur on end, his tail straight in the air.

Being interrupted by Silas,—for daily exercise and practise in the arts of being bitted and led about—never annoyed the colt. The calves and Caesar watched these performances, furtively, and wondered when their turns would come; True always told them the fun he had and took care to mention the subsequent reward of maple sugar.

For a short time a gentle pigeon came and sat between the young

12

horse's ears and cooed, softly, whilst he munched at his manger. This was agreeable to the sociable colt, but he was puzzled to notice that the bird did not like his other friend, the cat. True could see how tactfully Caesar tried to win the affections of the pigeon, even reaching out a paw to pat him sometimes.

One day his feathered friend did not come to the stable at the usual time and when the cat sauntered in that afternoon, with a look of keen content on his face, and a feather in his whiskers, True asked if he had seen the pigeon.

Caesar had not, of course!

He added, however, as he placidly washed the feather from his face, that "birds often flew away and did not return!" His expression was so sincere and sympathetic that the colt was no little comforted.

In spite of this treachery, Caesar was really fond of True, and brought him, from time to time, tokens of his affection in the way of delicacies—rats and mice he had caught in his stealthy rounds— sometimes a chicken's foot or a fish's head from the kitchen. It was difficult for True to refuse these cat-dainties without hurting Caesar's feelings, until he hit upon the clever expedient of pulling out a mouthful of delicious fodder from his rack and offering it in his turn to the cat!

One day the colt boasted to the cat that he "could see in the dark."

Caesar purred, contemptuously, washing his face the while.

"That, my friend," he said, "is a mere trifle, hardly worth bragging about! Now, if you could but speak the human language, then, indeed, would I wave my tail and meow, 'Hail, Master!'"

True was abashed, but said:

"Nay, my mother says speech is but a vain and doubtful good, especially in women!"

To this sally the cat had no reply, both he and Gipsey had known women better than the yearling True.

One day Silas brought a black lamb to the pasture, who at once made friends with the colt. The two romped and played together, much as human children might. For the timid little creature True came to have a deep attachment; he liked the feel of the warm little body against his leg. No doubt they exchanged ideas about things of interest as they listened to the brook, singing happily of woods and meadows through which it had run on its way to the river.

This sweet friendship lasted many days, but it was destined to end in a tragedy—one that must be related as it bore so directly upon the sudden awakening of some of the traits in the colt's character.

On the edge of a near-by forest there was a rude hut in which dwelt a family of outlaws who lived on their neighbors and left honest dealing to others. Round about the countryside it was whispered they were "Tories," and Gipsey told True the evil odor borne on the breeze from that direction was sufficient assurance that this was so; the outlaws were, indeed, British, and the wildest crew that ever stole a horse or fired a haystack!

One day, as True stood wrapt in thought beside the stream, admiring the courage that made it sing as happily in sunshine as in shadow, on dark days as on bright, Black Baby, as the lamb was called, came from the other side of the pasture and rubbed against his leg. Seeing in a moment that the colt was preoccupied, the lamb whisked away to wait for the usual whinney of invitation.

The Tory hut showed clear in the morning sunlight and, absently, a moment later the colt glanced that way. To his astonishment he saw the youngest boy, a ne'er-do-well who had stolen pumpkins and apples from his neighbors all his life, unloose a lean, gaunt dog and start towards the pasture.

This young fiend was, oddly enough, named William Howe, quite enough in itself to set an American by the ears! True recalled in a flash all his mother had told him of the British General of the same name.[2]

"How, now," he thought, "why comes the young robber this way?"

Black Baby continued to frisk about, trying to divert True from his serious mood. He sprang into the air and tossed his little head, cutting all manner of capers, but the colt did not seem inclined to join him in play.

William Howe climbed to the top of the stone fence and, balancing himself adroitly, gazed around as if to locate any possible mischief.

The dog sprang nimbly over and, yelping, ran after an innocent rabbit that bounded across the pasture like an India rubber ball, his short pennant making an almost unbroken line of white over the green grass as he fled before his enemy. Luckily he reached the opposite fence in time and darted behind the protecting stones; baffled, the dog stood barking, furiously.

Soon the boy put his fingers in his lips and whistled, shrilly.

Time and again True had warned Black Baby of this very dog, but the lamb, having known only love and kindness all his little life, forgot, and frolicked gaily towards him!

William Howe cried out in delight, "Sick him, Cornwallis!"

The cosset lamb stood an easy mark for the dog and in an instant lay gasping on the ground, the blood flowing from a horrid wound in his throat. His sobbing breath found an echo in True's heart and for the first time the colt lost control of himself.

Overcome with a thirst for vengeance, and, screaming as only a horse does when the strait is desperate, he plunged and reared. With a well-aimed blow of his hard, very dark, front-feet he knocked the dog senseless.

This did not satisfy the lamb's champion; he stamped the body of the wicked beast into the earth, crushing bones as if they had been straws! Furiously he bit, and finally caught the limp carcass in his strong teeth and threw it high in the air. For the moment he was a demon and sought, savagely, for more ways to wipe the remains out of existence!

Suddenly he remembered William Howe who stood at a distance, pelting him with stones. Uttering another fierce cry he turned upon the boy, baring his teeth hideously between his firm lips.

Howe made for the fence, where the desperate rabbit had sought cover, and scrambled over, thinking to be safe on the other side; he did not know the colt was descended from the "birds of the desert!"

True was not even *aware* of a barrier! As if he had wings he soared over it, doubling his hind-feet close under his body a little to one side.

A tree was all that saved the boy's life. Swinging up by a low-hanging branch, with the agility of a cat, he found himself out of breath and out of reach of the colt's gleaming teeth. From wide, scarlet nostrils the hot and excited breath of the maddened animal reached his bare feet.

The Tory scent that came down to True only increased his anger, but not being able to reach the boy, he resolved that the kicking he owed him could be postponed—for years, if necessary—but some day, *some day*, it would be delivered! Furthermore—he would kick nothing until that day arrived and he met this boy again on level ground!

How he kept his vow we shall see later.

FOOTNOTES:

[1] According to Joseph Battell. *Encyclopedia Britannica* says 1793.

15

[2] In 1776, Sir William Howe commanded an
army of 55,000 men in an effort to put down
"the wicked rebellion."

CHAPTER II.

TRUE IS BROKEN TO HARNESS.

Even, pleasant and cheerful was True's natural disposition, but besides these traits there were others that went to make up the peculiar perfection horse-flesh had attained in the twenty-five years before his birth.

A courage, vitality, and zest seemed to be in the very air of the world at that period of horse history, and the blend—through his father—of Arabian, Barb and Turk had produced in him the most ideal of horse characters.

That Southern strain was, no doubt, stimulated by the clear, bracing climate of New England, and the combination of circumstances which developed his muscles and expanded his chest, made him the fit founder of a race.

About the year he was born Eclipse, his kins-horse, died.

Eclipse was that four-footed bird "behind whom the whirlwind toiled in vain" and who, in his greatest race, "beat the other horse by two hundred yards, without urging!"[3]

Since then men have said that Eclipse ran "a mile a minute," but Gipsey told her son differently; she knew horses only ran against each other, not against time.

She also told the colt the part his family had played in the late War, and how General Washington, himself, had ridden one of them at Trenton; but she was obliged to confess, with a droop of her spirited tail, that his father, True Briton had, in his youth, served a British officer.

So graphic were some of these war-tales that the young horse quivered, and almost imagined he heard the crack of muskets and smelt the smoke of battle! He dreamed longingly of a time when he, too, might serve his country under the saddle of some brave soldier, and his nostrils grew wide and his eyes fiery at the hope which was so long afterwards to be realized.

Had she been a woman, and men had seen the workings of her mind as she instructed her son, Gipsey might have been called a witch and as such been burned. With pointing ears and ember-like eyes she neighed softly to him of the Desert; she seemed to hear its

17

call; to see its trackless wastes, and afar, at its limits, she told him groves of olive and date, and pools of clear, cool water lay.

One day, with that far-off look in her eyes, she said to him, prophetically:

"When other horses, now famous, are forgotten, my son, your memory will live on, your influence will still be felt. Men will still love you and you will be praised and revered by all who have knowledge of excellence in horse-flesh. A state will be noted for its horses, and Allah has chosen you to be the first of this line."

She told him to be ever brave, gentle, and loving; obedient to his master, Man; not to falter, not to turn back never mind the cost.

She told him how to anticipate a command, that he might obey, instantly, and he afterwards became so proficient in this sense that when he came to be trained to harness he obeyed Silas Whitman's every gesture, as if instinctively, often before the words themselves came. In later life, becoming more experienced, he often took the initiative in times of danger or peril.[4]

When True was a little over a year old Master Whitman brought a piebald horse to live in their stable. Poor old Ceph was of low birth and very stupid.

"In the Desert," Gipsey told him, "the Arabs say, 'if piebald, flee him as the pestilence, for he is own brother to a cow'!"

Ceph turned out to be a "stump-sucker" or "piper," and the grunts and groans accompanying his gnawing disturbed the other two horses intensely. At last when he began on the partition between his stall and True's it was too much for the colt to bear in silence and patience. He determined to cure him in some way, though at first he did not see how it was to be done.

One day, however, a bit of chain was left hanging on his manger and, when he pushed it with his nose, it made a jangling noise. Ceph, always curious, stopped his "cribbing" long enough to listen, dully, with his flapping ears, and to wonder what it was.

After a short time True found, to his surprise and satisfaction, that he could lift the chain with his teeth and, as he was now tall enough for his chin to reach the top of the partition, it occurred to him he could use the bit of iron to very good advantage.

He laid his plans accordingly and bade Caesar be on hand to see the fun.

About midnight Ceph began to gnaw.

Quick as wink True had the chain in his teeth and over the wall it went—crack—right between Ceph's floppy ears!

Such amazement there never was in any dull horse's quiet, stupid

18

mind! He squealed and sprang one side, startled into anger and affright. But when he recovered himself all was still; no suspicious noises came from his neighbor's stall.

Caesar had been standing on his hind legs, peeping through a hole in the partition and at sight of Ceph's bewilderment, he rolled over in a paroxysm of mirth, as if he did not have a bone in his body, while True stood motionless, guarding their secret.

Presently, very cautiously, Ceph began to gnaw again on the wood of his manger.

In his haste to give another lick, True nearly stepped on the prostrate cat, but, holding his foot poised a moment, Caesar sprang lightly from under it just as a mighty swing took the chain over the barrier.

Ceph threw his head into the air, indignantly, but his suspicions were unconfirmed the silence next door was so intense; then, to add to his perplexity, he heard Gipsey wake with a groan and a stamp.

"Will we never get any rest!" she neighed, hopelessly.

True whinneyed softly, over her side of his stable, to be of good cheer, the worst was over. And afterwards the least sound from Ceph brought a rattling of the mysterious chain which had struck him so hard on the head.

For a few nights this went on, but finally success crowned the colt's efforts and much to the satisfaction of all, Silas included, Ceph stopped gnawing.

This was not the only time True showed ingenuity. He learned many useful though not mischievous tricks all by himself, but it is not to be supposed that Silas thought as much of them as Gipsey. The colt discovered how to open all the gates, but, as he never thought to close them, their barn-companions wandered out and never returned without being sent for though the horses always came home in good temper after their wanderings in time for the evening meal. At last locks and keys were put on everything, and this was the first intimation True had that his pleasant little accomplishment was not appreciated by his master. As he grew older he eliminated the unpopular trick from his list.

One day, being thirsty, he began to consider how he could open the rain barrel, in which Mistress Whitman caught water for her washing. He tried hard to push the cover to one side, but some clever human contrivance made it catch, and so, after trying several other ways, he found the simple and right one of catching the handle in his strong young teeth and lifting straight upward!

Sometimes when he had done this and drunk all the water he

wanted, he would pick the cat up by the scruff of the neck with his teeth and hold him over the barrel, meowing desperately, for of all things Caesar hated water! True was only teasing him, but the cat never knew that, and a spasm of terror would chill his marrow at thought of being dropped in.

The death of Black Baby made True more serious and earnest. He went about his daily tasks with interest and spirit, but he did not romp so much and listened more attentively to his mother's teachings.

One day he found himself hitched up in harness with old Piebald, Ceph. Silas had thought Gipsey too spirited to begin him with, but True walked so fast, and—though very unsteadily at first—trotted so much faster than his mate that the next day he was taken out with his mother.

From her he had learned the Royal Road to Happiness and Success: "Obedience first, last, and all the time!"

It was, indeed, a proud day for the colt.

Easy it was for a horse to obey Silas Whitman, he was so careful to explain, and to be sure they understood; he never let them get fretted trying to find out what he wanted by themselves.

As soon as True found he was not expected to run or gallop in harness, he settled down to walking or trotting in his nervous brisk way, and soon the gaits of mother and son were evenly matched.

As time increased True became more and more lovable and people came for miles to see him; some even wanted to buy him and offered as much as twenty-five dollars. But Silas refused all offers for his pet. Very soon he was hitched to the "shay" alone. He stepped out bravely enough feeling the friendly hand of his master to advise and guide him. Then again he had a turn under the saddle; this was freer for there were not so many rules to remember!

When they went on trips of the latter kind, Silas, who was a very well-informed man, talked to him and told him many interesting things and gave him much instruction. Sometimes, on their way home over open fields, grassy knolls and wooded hillsides, Silas would take the wrong turning and leave True to find out the right way by himself. That strange sense of direction in horses was singularly acute in True and they invariably reached home safely, the horse enjoying this confidence of his rider.

One sunny day when the little horse was nearly two years old, they were returning from a trip up the river when Silas swooned, it was a sickness to which he was subject, and, slipping from the saddle to the road, he rolled into the ditch. True, no little disturbed, stood thoughtful a moment, wondering what he could do for his unconscious friend. Finally he caught hold of the Continental collar with his teeth and drew him gently up on the grassy border of the road, under the shade of an oak. Looking around he whinneyed for help, but, as no answer came, he turned and galloped homeward, nor did he go by the longer way of the road. Over rough, uneven, cleared spaces, he went; stone fences stretched across his way; here and there strips of dense woods interfered with but did not retard his speed or intention.

When he neared the house a curl of blue smoke told him where he would find Mistress Whitman, nor was he mistaken. He trotted straight to the kitchen window at which he was wont to receive goodies from her generous hands; there she stood, slender and womanish, beside a pot of soup, hanging on the crane, whose warm fragrance permeated the air.

True whinneyed sharply. She looked up, and, seeing the empty saddle, started with anxiety and hastened out. The horse rubbed his nose on her sleeve and neighed his message, softly.

She seemed to understand the horse-language at once and, leading him to the horse-block, climbed into the saddle without delay.

And this was True's first experience of carrying a lady! She was so light of weight, and she spoke to him so fearlessly, that he drew much comfort through his bridle-rein. He started off at an even canter not hesitating at his stable door, though it must have been hard to pass the appetizing sound of Gipsey and Ceph munching at their supper.

This time he took the road, in a long smooth gait, and after a short time reached the strip of woods where Silas had been left.

Master Whitman, thin and very bright of eye, was sitting up now, and seemed much better, so his good wife aided him to mount the horse and climbed up behind him; thus they set out toward home, and True had his first experience of "carrying double."

What a supper the "pony" had that night!

Oats, dry as pease, corn and carrots, a little flaxseed jelly, and chopped hay springled with salt.

'Twas a supper fit for Eclipse, himself!

FOOTNOTES:

[3] *Eclipse and O'Kelly*, page 88; Theodore An-

21

drea Cook, M. A., F. S. A.

[4] In 1891 President Harrison attended a meeting of The Association of Road and Trotting Horse Breeders, at White River Junction, Vermont. In the course of his remarks on that occasion he said: "I understand that it was so arranged that after I had seen the flower of manhood and womanhood in Vermont I should be given an exhibition of the next grade in intelligence and worth in the State—your good horses. I had, recently, through the intervention of my Secretary of War, the privilege of coming into possession of a pair of Vermont horses. They are all I could wish for, and, as I said the other day at the little village from which they came, they are of good Morgan stock, of which some one has said, 'their greatest characteristic is that they enter into consultation with the driver, or rider, whenever there is a difficulty.'"— *The Morgan Horse, page 27, Joseph Battell.*

CHAPTER III.

CEPH'S UNHAPPY FATE.

Never had Ceph been treated kindly by anyone; he'd never had "half a chance in life," as Gipsey said. Nobody ever praised him, everybody blamed him, and he had nothing but blows and hard words for his portion. Even his food, which always came irregularly, had to be gobbled, for fear time enough to eat it comfortably would not be given him! Nobody ever rubbed him down when he was hot and tired, and his work was harder and more exacting than that of the other two.

For the most part he took it philosophically, with only an occasional groan until, perhaps, he saw better food measured out for his neighbors than was measured out for him, then he stamped and grunted and sometimes bit at them, crossly.

For many years he had been subject to spavin, at times his hock swelled badly and he went lame and limped painfully. At last Silas could close his eyes no longer to the fact that unless something were done for the old horse he would become entirely useless.

In Springfield a horse doctor lived who knew, among other things, how to "fire" a spavined hock. True had once seen this man thrust a sharp knife into a horse's mouth who had lampers; the flow of warm red blood had made the colt shudder and, remembering this, he was very sorry when he found out this cruel person was to visit Ceph.

Gipsey recalled that this Dr. Quack had once been sent for to see a neighbor's suffering cow; he arrived, looking wise and solemn, and declared the cow had a disease called "hollow-horn." He thereupon split her tail lengthwise and filled the raw opening with salt and pepper.[5]

The poor cow died, and none but her barn-mates knew the distressing fact that she had really died of "hollow stomach," not "hollow horn," because their owner was so cruelly economical with food!

It was with no little sorrow that True recognized the coarse, rasping voice of the "doctor" when he came to see Ceph late one evening.

Through a crack in their darkening stalls True espied the red-hot crow-bar, and the guttering tallow dip Silas had lighted and brought from the kitchen.

Piebald Ceph had always been a mild-tempered horse, but scarce had the firing-iron touched his hock than he sent it—and the candle—flying into the hayloft, with an unexpected and well-directed kick.

Before a horse could have whinneyed the place was in flames, the dry hay dropping in blazing bunches from overhead.

A diabolic scene followed!

Seconds passed like hours.

True jerked his halter loose in terror, snapping the rope sharply; his heart almost ceased to beat, he was so frightened. Gipsey, locked in her stall, uttered a scream, as horses sometimes do when overcome with fear: old Ceph, crowding into the extreme corner of his stable, groaned pitifully.

It was like a roaring furnace, the heat intense, the smoke suffocating.

The shouting of the men was drowned in the confused mingling of horrible sounds as the flames leaped and licked the dry hay and caught the well-seasoned timbers.

The horrid odor of burnt hair, a sudden silence in Ceph's stall, told a heart-rending tale. The echoes of his mother's cry had hardly died away when True felt a cool, wet cloth thrown over his eyes and held tightly; something struck him violently, and a voice spoke to him in such a tone of command that he forgot everything and, trembling like a leaf, allowed himself to be led into the outer air.

Then, vaguely at first, he recognized Mistress Whitman's tones, soothing now, and tender, albeit very shaky!

"Come, my little pet, there's naught to fear now!"

And, trusting her, the colt followed tractably enough as she led him up two stone steps into the kitchen and took the bandage from his eyes.

Then she hurried out, closing the door tight.

An awful crash, a sudden greater roar, then ominous silence—the barn roof had fallen in!

"Alas, my poor mother!" groaned True.

The rattling of a tin pan at his side made him turn; to his everlasting joy he saw Gipsey, safe and sound as himself, shut up in the kitchen.

Gipsey was an excitable mare, and began to prance about the place in an unseemly way, switching kettles and pewter pots off the table with her nervous tail and knocking them to the floor with a monstrous racket.

Finally she pushed the cover from the swinging pot on the crane. Luckily the fire had been out some time and the delicious contents of the pot barely warm, else she would have had her nose burned. The odor of the mash proved very enticing and she was greedily, or maybe thoughtlessly, about to drink it all, when True pushed her one side, as if to remind her of her manners, and finished it himself—little dreaming, either one of them, it was the Whitman's frugal supper.

During their feast the uproar outside had subsided, and in a little while Silas and his wife came in, saying it was all over with poor old Ceph.

The noses of the two rescued horses were gray and greasy with the rich mash, but in the thankfulness of their escape the Whitmans cared nothing for that. Mistress Whitman put her cheek against True's soupy face and sobbed in a very womanish way for joy at his being spared to them.

The young horse submitted patiently to her caresses, though her hair, looking like dry, crisp hay, smelled mortally of smoke; he saw it was a comfort to her woman-heart to hang about his neck and murmur softly in his ear:

"True, dear little horse," she whispered. "It doesn't matter about Ceph."

"There it is again," thought True. "Nobody cares whether poor old Ceph is burnt up or not."

And nobody did, as long as Gipsey and he were saved.

FOOTNOTES:

[5] Once a common practice among the negroes of the South.

CHAPTER IV.

JUSTIN MORGAN.

In True's third year, Master Whitman came one morning, betimes, to brush him down before taking him out for his usual exercise—so the "pony" thought. But after a while he was convinced that his master called him names more loving and tender than usual and that his voice had a sorrowful ring.

Gipsey and True knew that hard times had come knocking at the farm-gate and that their kind master was in debt because his crops had failed the year before. They knew, too, if the worst came to the worst they might have to be sold to pay these debts.

On this particular morning Master Whitman murmured sadly to his pet as he continued to polish the sides of his symmetrical body until they shone like the bosom of the river when the afternoon sunlight played upon it; and his heavy mane and tail were brushed until they waved lightly under every passing breeze.

With unfailing intuition the colt saw the future: their happy home, alas, was about to be broken up. Even Caesar felt the prevailing gloom; dejectedly, he sat on a beam and washed his face for the fifth time that morning, though it was but just sunrise.

Gipsey peered over the partition of their stall and whinneyed softly, but with resignation, for, wise old horse that she was, she knew it was the lot of horses to be parted, sooner or later—here today, there to-morrow.

Presently the cat sprang nimbly down, and arching his back, rubbed himself against his master's leg and purred with sympathy.

In spite of a certain sadness, True himself felt no little excitement—anticipating adventure, as is the manner of youth first starting out into the great world. He did not then know the horrors of homesickness from which affectionate horses suffer so keenly—suffering that neither sugar nor salt can assuage.

Master Whitman had always made play and pleasure of training, and had never given True a task he could not perform. For this reason the horse accepted every order unhesitatingly, with the confidence of absolute trust. They had become so endeared to one another for these and sundry other causes that the idea of a parting was inexpressibly saddening to both.

When, a half hour later, True was hitched to the "shay"—which he now pulled with such ease and pleasure—he fared forth, sad at heart, but eager and brisk in gait, as usual. The day had advanced and, as they travelled, the river glinted gold in the light which the morning sun threw over the fringe of trees along its banks. Very soon they arrived at the tavern where already several teams stood waiting.

Throwing the reins loosely on the horse's back—for he had been trained to stand without hitching—Silas Whitman sprang from the "shay" and entered the tavern.

He was gone the best part of an hour, and when he returned he was not alone. A tall, slender stranger walked beside him, and as they drew near the colt perceived from the odor of this man that he was a pleasant-tempered person and friendly to animals.

Indeed, True liked him at once, and 'twas well, for the pale, scholarly looking man whose name he would one day bear, was none other than *Justin Morgan*, who had once lived in Springfield, but had moved to Randolph, Vermont, in 1788, with his family.

As Master Morgan pressed the muscles of the young horse the latter did not flinch nor draw away. Then the mouth had to be examined and the feet looked at, one by one. Questions had to be answered and other investigations made, common among men engaged in a horse deal.

Master Whitman answered the questions, or stood in grave silence, his eyes moist with the tears he could not entirely hide, as his acquaintance considered True's various traits.

"Yes, sir," the stranger finally said, "this colt, as you say, is free from natural blemish and is not disfigured by that cruel, prevailing practice of branding. He seems sound.... You say he is the son of De Lancey's True Briton, and his mother a descendant of the Layton Barb?"

"I repeat it," replied Silas Whitman, *"these are the facts, to the best of my belief."*

He could scarcely trust himself to speak.

"He is remarkably well ribbed-up and firm under the mane, for so young a horse," said Master Morgan, "but he is small."

"He is not yet entirely developed," was the answer. "You see, he is, as yet, scarce three years old. But he is a bit over fourteen hands, and weighs already upwards of nine hundred pounds. I told you he might be called a pony, except for his characteristics."

"No doubt he will increase in weight, and maybe a bit in height," Master Morgan agreed. "His Arabian ancestry would account for his size. Not that I am one of those foolish persons who considers size necessary for *perfection*," he hastily added. "Since I have seen him I am willing to take him in place of the twenty-five dollars you owe me, though twenty-five dollars is a large sum, and I am a poor man. Shall we call it settled?"

For a moment True thought his old master would surely have one of his spells of faintness, but when he finally spoke his voice was brave and steady.

"The pony," he said, gently, "will be ready for you in the morning." He rested his arm across True's neck, while the stranger looked away for a moment. "This little horse," Silas continued, after a pause, having recovered himself, "has been to me what the 'steed of the desert' is to his Arab master. When I part with him I give you the best friendship I ever had; the best work of three years, spent in training and developing the intelligence of this remarkable horse. And, mark you, he will live to bear out the confidence I have in him. I have ever treated him as a human being; I have romped with him, played with him, talked to him as I might have talked to a child—if Providence had blessed my wife and me with such a treasure—but I have ever insisted upon *obedience* and *respect*, as a father should insist upon these qualities from a child."

"As I insist upon in mine," acquiesced Master Morgan, as Silas hesitated a moment, feeling he was perhaps saying too much.

"There is but one thing more I would add," went on Silas, feeling a friendly sympathy from Master Morgan. "Be good to him and he will be faithful to you, teach him to love you and his willing service will be to you and yours until the end. He does not know what falter means, and if you are wise you will never let him find out by asking him to do impossible things. Ask of him only that which is within his power and he will never fail you."

Kind-hearted Master Morgan grasped Whitman's hand. "I shall not forget," he said, deeply touched.

That night Caesar climbed on the rack of True's stall and dropped lightly down on the horse's back, where he purred an undying affection and sorrow at his friend's approaching departure. Hoping to cheer him a little, the cat told many anecdotes of other stables and barns which he suggested True might some time visit, but the heavy sadness could not be lifted from their hearts. Gipsey gave him advice, and at midnight Master Whitman came to see if all were well with his pet. At cock-crow Mistress Whitman appeared with a most delicious breakfast as a parting favor.

Silas had just finished rubbing the young horse down when his new owner came, bringing his own saddle and bridle—and very easy and comfortable they were, too.

When the sad partings were over, True stepped fearlessly out on his way to the broad highway of the world, where he was to have so many sweet and bitter experiences.

CHAPTER V.

TRUE MEETS HIS FATHER.

"'Oh, 'twas a joyful sound to hear,
Our tribes devoutly say,
Up Israel, to the Temple haste,
And keep your festal day!'"

It was Justin Morgan, singing his favorite hymn, in his light tenor voice, and True pointed his ears to better hear the agreeable sound.

Master Morgan was not a strong man physically, and his ways were those of a scholar and student, but he was lovable and staunch and true, and, lilting the stave of "Mear" he set out on the road to the southward.

Along the bank of the tranquil river stretched the highway to Hartford, and it was Master Morgan's plan to exhibit his new horse at the great fair so soon to be held in that fine city.

It was near sunset when they arrived, and True stepped out so smartly, and Justin Morgan, being a great rider, the people paused in the streets to admire them, as they cantered easily on to the public stable to rest and refresh themselves.

True's name was now changed to "Figure," the name once borne by a famous horse, dead some years since; and under this name he came to be known through the columns of that very respected paper, *The Hartford Courant*.

"Next to his own father, sir," True heard the hostler say, as he led him into a stall and snapped the catch of the halter into the ring. "Now what do you think of that? The horse in the next box, sir, is Mr. Selah Norton's Beautiful Bay, him that was True Briton."

Master Morgan looked in at the splendid animal and said, "Oh, the De Lancey horse, eh? A fine fellow he is still, I see, in spite of his age. Well, all I can say is, mine is the 'worthy son of a worthy sire'!"

True quivered. Already the great world was offering adventure and reward. Crowding through his veins the fire of his father's race throbbed and surged, his mane shook and he flicked his waving tail with eager anticipation. His alert ears pointed back and forth with attention, his eyes glowed and his wide nostrils trembled as he inhaled the scent of his father for the first time. Proud and vigorous, he pawed the floor to attract Beautiful Bay; now and then he glanced with feigned carelessness through a wide crack.

Full soon he was rewarded by a sight of the gleaming eye of his neighbor at the same aperture.

For a moment they gazed in silence; then True took a step forward, and raising his nose to the top of the partition met the firm tip of his father's.

Without further demonstration an affection sprang up between the two.

In the course of time the hostler came to lead the new horse out, in the deepening twilight, to show him to some visitors. The interest True took in the performance, one could be reasonably certain, was not on account of the visitors, but because he was well aware of his splendid father's interest and admiration.

That night when all was quiet the old war-horse said:

"You are like your mother, my son, I remember her well—and a fine, noble mare she was, to be sure. Her hoof beat music from the path and she struck the road with the same nervous tread that I see you have—as a pigeon in full career repulses the air. She scoffed at hills and mounted them with a dash of spirited flight, as if she joyed in their difficulties."

True recalled his mother's admiration of his father, and his heart beat gratefully at these words. He, too, remembered Gipsey's poetic motion, her rhythmic step, as if she trod an even melody, and her willingness to take a hill.

* * * *

"As his name is, so is he,
If you believe not, come and see!"

So *The Hartford Courant* described Beautiful Bay, and the rhyme was a by-word about the town—for they were very proud of Beautiful Bay in Hartford. It was not long before True heard the couplet in the stables, and right proud was he to be the son of so praised a father.

Beautiful Bay told True many stirring tales in the quiet nights they spent so close together, for the older horse had ever been a "soldier of Fortune" and his life one of constant change and excitement.

It was a great boast for a horse to say he had been bred in the

31

De Lancey stables, for those De Lanceys, like Mahommed, had been lovers of horses, and their stables and half-mile running track, in the centre of what was so soon to be the very heart of the great city of New York, was the finest in the Northern Colonies before the War of the Revolution.

Gay blades were those De Lanceys, and their rightful inheritance was the sporting blood of old England, though they were, after all, part Huguenot, part Dutch, by ancestry.

Colonel De Lancey, True Briton's first owner, had married a Mistress Van Courtlandt, whose family had a King and a Bishop at their backs, and occupied half the important posts under the crown. He was a rollicking, generous, reckless gentleman, at home alike in drawing room or on the course, but when, through stress of circumstances, this British officer had to change his mode of living, there was a sale of his horses at John Fowler's Tavern, near the Tea-Water Pump, in Bowery Lane. All the favorites went but his especial saddle horse, True Briton—who now frankly admitted to his son his worth and beauty in those days. Indeed, he seemed to have no *false modesty* about it at all, and confessed his superiority over all his stable-mates, even though among them there were such horses as Lath and Slamerkin.

According to the accounts of the old horse his youth had been spent in a time the like of which True could never see. He told of the gaily dressed dandies—waiting on ladies in silks and satins and waving plumes—at the meets; of the sudden seal of disapproval Congress had put upon the dissipations and extravagances of the race-course; of how the Annapolis Jockey Club had set the foolish fashion of economy by closing its course; of how the grass grew up in the one-time splendid Centre Course at Philadelphia.

But of all his anecdotes the tale of how True Briton became a true Patriot interested the young horse most, and ran in this wise:

Colonel De Lancey was stationed at Westchester with his regiment, which was known far and wide as "The Cow-Boys," because they stole cattle from the "Skinners" (a name given the farmers at that time).

At last the latter resolved to appeal to the Colonel-in-command for a protection of their rights and property. Accordingly, "Skinner Smith" called upon Colonel De Lancey, a white handkerchief tied to a stick, to show a peaceful errand, and made complaint of the depredations of the "Cow-Boys."

Now the Colonel, ever cool and gay, as became a De Lancey, cried out with a great laugh:

"These be the chances of war, my lack-beard. If my good sol-diers need cattle, or food of other kind, and you will not give it to them, egad! they must steal it! Best curb your uncouth tongue and be gone!"

"Then, by my lack of beard!" quoth Skinner Smith, nettled—he was an impudent young scamp, and feared no one—"'What is sauce for the goose, is sauce for the gander!' If these be the 'chances of war,' look well to that fine horse of yours! I warn you fairly, others can be cattle stealers, too! I warn you fairly—and now wish you a very good day."

It chanced that under cover of darkness one night, shortly after-ward, Colonel De Lancey rode to see his mother at some distance and left True Briton hitched at the door-step.

Young Smith, waiting his "chance of war," sprang from behind a tree as the door of the house closed, unhitched the horse, leaped into the saddle and plunging spurs into True Briton's sides—who, wide of eye and red-nostrilled, sprang forward—did not draw rein until he was well within the American lines.

The amazed and disgusted Colonel raised an alarm and roused his orderlies, but too late. He never saw his favorite again until one fine day he found himself incarcerated in the jail at Hartford with many another "Red-Coat."

Beautiful Bay, then in the possession of Mr. Selah Norton, was standing in front of Bull's Tavern, across Meeting House Green.

"Blood will tell, in men as well as horses," finished Beautiful Bay. "When Colonel De Lancey recognized me he threw me a laughing greeting and a wave of the hand. I could almost hear what his parted lips were saying: 'The chance of war, my friend!'"

CHAPTER VI.

TRUE GAZES UPON MISTRESS LLOYD, OF MARYLAND.

The following day, laughter and talk outside the stable announced that several persons had come to visit the horses.

It chanced that among them was that brilliant quartette of men, known as the "Hartford Wits," with Master Trumbull at their head.

The latter stood chatting with a mere slip of a girl, dark-eyed and merry. In her hand she carried a fine, thread-lace kerchief— like gossamer films at dawn—and a pouf of gauze fell away from her snowy throat. She wore a perriot of flowered taffeta trimmed with herrisons, and from beneath her petticoat two little slippered feet peeped shyly. She was the most radiant being True had ever seen. Enraptured, he followed her with his eyes whichever way she turned. For all her beauty, she was yet strong and fine in her promise of fuller womanhood. There was a quick certainty about her every movement, and a steadiness of eye that showed no indeterminate character.

Near her stood a Coxcomb, filling the air with odors of musk and powders, offensive to the nostrils of the little horse who was led past him. A secret loathing for this popinjay was born in his heart which he never outgrew.

"Ah, Mistress Lloyd," said the Coxcomb, drawling his words disagreeably, and waving a scented lace-bordered handkerchief, "what say you to Beautiful Bay? Have your kinsmen, Carroll of Carrollton, or the Hon. Edward Lloyd—or, for the matter of that, the dashing Tom Dulaney—anything finer at their country-seats in Maryland? Is there anything in Virginia, or South Carolina, to compare with our Beautiful Bay?"

Smiling, the maid stepped in front of Beautiful Bay and held out a slender pink palm—like the petals of wild roses True had seen on his way from Springfield—on it lay a bit of maple sugar, and right proudly the old horse arched his neck and ate from her hand, picking up the crumbs with his firm but flexible lips, that his hard teeth might not scar the tender flesh.

With her dainty kerchief she flicked his side lightly, replying evasively:

"We've nothing *better groomed*." Turning to her father she cried gaily, "Come hither, Daddy, dear, and touch his satin coat!"

Beautiful Bay pranced a little to show his appreciation.

"Have a care, my child," warned her father.

Her laughter rippled forth as she drew Beautiful Bay's muzzle down for a caress.

"It would not bite a maiden's cheek, would it?" she cooed in his ready ear, and he trembled with joy at the sound. Young Mistress Lloyd's "way with horses" was known from Maryland to Boston.

The Coxcomb flicked his riding boot impatiently with his whip. This annoyed Beautiful Bay, who, thinking to please the maid, turned abruptly to him and bared his teeth, flattening his ears.

The popinjay sprang to one side.

"He can't abide smells!" explained the hostler, apologetically, as he led the old horse back into his stable.

And this was the first time that True saw Mistress Lloyd, of Maryland; though she had taken no notice of him, he never forgot it.

Deeply attached did the two horses become to each other, and Old Worldly-Wise taught Young Innocence much that was afterwards of use to him. He told him of the city, where men sat, far into the night, and played cards or other games by the glare of torchlight or wax candle; of how they danced with or serenaded fair ladies till cock-crow. It contrasted strangely with True's former quiet nights and peaceful days in the Valley of the Connecticut, but it interested him intensely and awakened longings within him.

He marvelled to see Beautiful Bay active and spirited enough at his age to clear a five-barred gate like a greyhound, and to see his bearing under the saddle alike youthful and stylish.

The old horse had a fund of anecdotes to impart about the Desert and its traditions.

"Arabs," he said, "think it wicked to change their coursers into beasts of burden and tillage. Why did Allah make the ox for the plough and the camel to transport merchandise, if not that the horse was for the race?"

True had no answer ready, so Beautiful Bay continued:

"If you meet one of the Faithful in the Desert mounted on a *kochlani*, and he shall say to you, 'God bless you!' before you can say, 'And God's blessing be upon you!' he shall be out of sight."

True learned how to judge a horse by his color through Arabian tradition.

"White is for princes, but these do not stand the heat; black brings good fortune, but fears rocky ground; chestnut is most active—if one tells you he has seen a horse 'fly in the air,' and the horse be chestnut, believe him!"

There was a pause, during which True anxiously waited to hear what was said of bays.

Finally he asked.

"They say," answered his father, with a certain natural pride, "that 'bay is hardiest and best.' If one tells you he has seen a horse 'leap to the bottom of a precipice without hurting himself,' and if he say 'bay,' believe him!"

And being bay, True was happy.

"The Arab," continued the father, "who lives with his horse, and prizes him above his family, as is most meet and proper, learns to know him well. There are those in the Desert to-day who claim to trace the lineage of their horses back to those of Mohammed. These they train to endure hunger, fatigue and thirst to stand the Desert life. Some are said to be able to travel eighty leagues in twenty-four hours."

There were modern incidents in Beautiful Bay's lore—tales of the Southern States—so lately colonies—told him by his famous father, Traveller, who was imported from England and owned by Colonel Tayloe of Virginia.

"The blood of a thoroughbred flows quicker on the course than on a hill-side farm," said the old horse, and related a story of the meet at Annapolis, when he and Colonel De Lancey went down from New York to visit The Dulaney of Maryland.

Discussing the merits of the horses stood a group of the famous horsemen of the day: Tom Lee, of Virginia; Mason, of Gunstan Hall, and De Lancey, of New York—when The Dulaney joined them.

"'Sdeath, De Lancey!" he cried, in his hearty voice, "and right glad am I to see you here. These spindling bets of fifty or a hundred pounds please me not. I want gold, man, gold, I say!" Laughing carelessly, he flicked a speck of dust from his coat sleeve with a white linen handkerchief.

"Gold? Egad, so do I!" answered the rollicking De Lancey. "What say you to a *peck* of gold? Neither do I deal in quarters and halves."

"Make it a struck *bushel* of Spanish dollars, and I will back my horse against yours or the field!" cried the Southerner.

The bet made was perhaps the most sensational money-bet ever made on the Annapolis course.

Deafening cheers rent the air as The Dulaney's horse finished the one-mile circle a nose ahead.

CHAPTER VII.

IN WHICH MISTRESS LLOYD, OF MARYLAND, GIVES TRUE HIS FIRST RIBBAND.

One sunny September morning, when the weather was clear and fine and the trees were waving their crisp, gay-tinted leaves over the grass-bordered roadways leading to the fair-grounds, the horses were blanketed and led towards the place of exhibition, for this was the great opening of the Hartford Fair, and many had come from as far as New York and Boston to attend it. There was much prancing and side-stepping among the horses after a fine breakfast to put them in a good humor.

True had been exhibited once at a small fair in Springfield and knew a little of what was expected of him, but of course this was a much greater occasion and a sensation of slight nervousness and anticipation held his heart.

Some of the younger horses were ill-mannered; they bit at their grooms or snorted and showed their teeth rudely, which astonished True, for he had been taught to be polite always. Some of them grew very excited and some knew they might change owners, and receive prizes for this trait or that. It was a day long to be remembered by them all.

What a scene met their eyes when, at last, they were in sight of the Grounds! Early, as it was, there were more men assembled together than True had ever seen and they made a point of all talking at once, which confused the horses no little; they shouted at the tops of their voices, too, as if everybody were stone deaf.

The women, however, stood quietly, and modestly at one side in little sheltered booths where they displayed in a most becoming manner their handiwork: quilts, with beautiful and appropriate names, and wonderful pieces of hand-woven homespun and linen. Farther on True espied piles of carrots, squashes and other delicious things which would have made his mouth water had he not been so bewildered by the noises. Music sounded and set him dancing and showing his remarkable muscles to advantage.

Even Beautiful Bay, experienced as he must have been in such events, seemed to be under the influence of the lively atmosphere and curved his neck with spirit to the admiration and respect of everyone who knew the old horse. True felt a little anxiety for the result when Beautiful Bay was led before the Judges, but this was quite unnecessary; he returned with a blue ribband on his bridle and a very satisfied look in his eye.

Then the Three-year-olds were called.

True's temples throbbed; there were many beautiful horses there and, being modest, he had not guessed that he was the most beautiful and meritorious of them all.

When they were led out some bared their teeth, kicked at each other, and misbehaved shockingly. The contrast between True's breeding and theirs was very marked. When the Judges approached some of them even went so far as to whirl for a kick!

True in his turn, however, stepped out briskly and easily, small, lean head high, heavy black mane and tail waving lightly in the morning breeze. But, all suddenly, the stupid groom jerked his halter sharply.

Startled, the young horse flung himself backward.

"Now, you young rascal!" cried the lout, grandly, as if he were Mahommed himself, "None of your capers with *me*!"

Not being accustomed to rudeness, True backed, indignantly, and dragged the boy along with him.

At this moment there was a rustle, like leaves in autumn, or the brush of wings, and the flying figure of a maid seemed poised beside the little horse, so light and airy was she.

All the odors of aromatic herbs and grasses of Arabia—myrrh, frankincense and balsam, of which his mother had told him—enveloped his imagination and delighted his senses. He thrust his large tremulous nostrils forward, hungry to inhale more deeply of this new creature. Never had he scented her like before.

"Oh, please, Mr. Judge!" she cried, and as soon as she spoke True recognized the dulcet tones of Mistress Lloyd, of Maryland. Thrilling, as she caught his rein, he calmed himself instantly. "Don't let them jerk him so! Ah, my Beauty," she continued, putting her cheek against his, "here is a piece of sugar for you!" She extended the rose-leaf palm, from which he had seen his father eat one day and on which was another bit of maple sugar. "See, he is so *willing* to be good, *if you will but let him*!"

When he had lipped her hand all over very gently, to get the last crumb, True poked his small muzzle into the hollow of her neck and listened to her voice murmuring in his ear. All the soft breezes and blue sky of the universe were concentrated in the delicious spell of her presence, for this young maiden was one of those rare human beings who possess a mysterious understanding of animals, especially horses, which gives a power and control over them—almost miraculous.

True stepped carefully, lest his small well-shaped hoofs might tread upon the marvellously tiny feet half hidden beneath the flowered petticoat. All the while her voice was saying soft, delightful things in his listening ear.

When she finally gave up his rein and turned away, the young horse followed, drawn as by a magnet and dragged the groom with him, scarce seeming to feel the boy pulling at the halter.

A murmur of polite laughter made Mistress Lloyd look back.

Smiling sweetly, she turned and stroked True's broad forehead with her magic hand, and, telling him softly, to "go back and be judged," she reminded him he was at a Fair.

Indeed he needed reminding, for so absorbed had he been in her loveliness that he had forgotten all else!

The groom then gave a gentler tug at the halter and True consented to be led before the Judges, who had not yet told the people he was the finest Three-year-old in New England. "The Hartford Wits" and their friends, the Maryland Lloyds, watched the consultation of Judges, hoping the ribband would be given to "Figure."

In a few moments one of the committee came and spoke a few words to Mistress Lloyd; she smiled with pleasure, and nodded her pretty head in assent.

In another moment True heard the sound as of leaves in an autumn forest, and there she was, beside him once more, a fillet of blue in her hand.

Daintily she reached the headstall of his halter and firmly she tied it on—all the while talking to him, oh, so sweetly:

"And so 'tis yours! I knew 'twould be, you beauty! You're far lovelier than your father, even, and you must always be a good colt and make everybody love you as you've made me!"

Somehow, True did not mind being called a "colt" by her, it seemed more like a caress than patronage; but had the *Coxcomb*, standing by, done it he would have been tempted to take a whirl at him.

"Some day," went on Mistress Lloyd, "my father will buy you for me and I shall take you down to Maryland—I want Tom Dulaney to see you!" True could hear by the tones of her voice as she mentioned his name that this *Tom Dulaney* must be a personage of consequence. "You are small, and some might say not lean enough to hunt, but you are the dearest animal I ever won the love of!" For 'twas ever the habit of this fair maid to weave her spell over animals, and well aware was she of their response!

Then, oh, miracle of delights! as she finished tying the strand she kissed his straight face with lips that looked and smelled like crimson clover blossoms wet with dew.

This perfumed dream was broken by a disagreeable laugh, and a well-bred but none the less offensive voice said:

"The brute will bite you, Mistress."

It was the Coxcomb speaking.

"I am afraid of no horse living, Master Knickerbocker," she gave reply, quietly; then looking straight at him, she finished, "horses are often truer than men."

She turned quickly and joined her father.

CHAPTER VIII.

TRUE GOES TO FOUND HIS RACE.

Beautiful Bay boasted of having carried the Marquis de Lafayette to the great banquet the Hartford people gave him at the Bunch of Grapes Tavern, in 1784. The reference to this made the younger horse hope, as ever, rather recklessly, that another war might be declared which would give him such opportunities to distinguish himself as his father had had.

Sometimes father and son stood beneath the Elm on Main street and Beautiful Bay told True of the meeting there of Generals Washington, Hamilton and Knox, in 1780, when they discussed the Yorktown campaign. The ground under it was trodden hard, as if many others had stood to tell or listen to the story.

One day True heard the tale of the Charter Oak as they passed it on their way for a lounge on Sentinel Hill; and he heard, too, the exciting times accompanying the burning of the State House, in 1783.

Often they passed a queer looking young man; head bent in thought, hands clasped behind his back, at whom people pointed, saying with a shrug of understanding, as if to make allowances for the eccentricities of a scholar.

"There goes No-y Webster!"

Now and again the two horses went over to Mathew Allyn's mill where the stones turned corn into delicious meal; or they made trips under the saddle up Rocky Hill, where men were hanged from a gibbet over the precipice if they had been wicked—or if men *said* they had—which came to the same thing in the end.

Certain days each week were called "Market Days," and farmers came to Hartford to sell their produce. The Meeting House bell called them together and when True was present they often stood near to admire him and invite him to visit their farms. These were very profitable experiences to True and his owner, for there was always plenty of good food and bedding.

It was with no little regret, therefore, that True found one day Master Morgan was making ready to leave, and he must say goodbye to his father and friends in that pleasant town.

Nevertheless, when they set out, and turned their faces northward, he stepped out with a stout heart, remembering his mother's instruction:

"Duty that we cheerfully do,
Is always quickest through!"

The highway they took was the one they had travelled when on their way to Hartford, and True's spirits rose, thinking he might soon see his dear mother and Caesar. He would have so much to tell them of his experiences in the great world.

A feeling of keen content and happiness swept over him as he cantered easily along the banks of the stately Connecticut River, or stopped to graze on the rich abundant grass bordering the roadway.

'Twas at turn of day he felt a sweet nearness to his old home, and by a thousand familiar signs and senses he knew they were approaching. Plucking up all his courage and enthusiasm, he increased his speed and, almost breathless with joy, stopped at the familiar barn-door and whinneyed twice in the old way.

There was no response.

His heart sank; a sudden anxiety seized him.

Finally Caesar appeared and purred a soft welcome as he rubbed against his old friend's leg. True made hurried enquiries as to his mother's welfare, while Master Morgan gave "halloo!" for the inmates of the house.

"Alas," mewed the cat, sitting down to wash his face, "things have changed since you went away. Your mother is sold into the South——"

"Into the South!" interrupted True, but Caesar saw nothing exciting in that, and continued, placidly:

——"and our master lies ill of the fever, our mistress ever at his side and no one to notice *me* at all. The stables are lonely, even the rats and mice have moved away for lack of food, for the garden and farm are grown up in weeds." And he wiped his paw surreptitiously across his eye, curled himself up on a beam and fell asleep.

The responsive tears filled True's eyes, and he would have roused the cat with other questions but at the moment Mistress Whitman opened the kitchen door. She offered Master Morgan friendly greeting, but when she caught sight of True she ran quickly out and threw her arms about his neck. Her old pet was equally glad to see her and thrust his muzzle into the folds of the white kerchief about her neck and made little affectionate sounds of greeting in reply.

"Come, True, little pony," she whispered, "he has almost grieved himself to death at parting from you. The very sight of you will make him better."

Without ado, she led the horse right up the two stone steps and into the kitchen where once he and his mother had stolen soup out of the pot which was even now swinging from the crane. As he recalled the incident he thrust his wide nostrils forward, but, smiling sadly, Mistress Whitman drew him to the inner door. His shod hoofs made an unseemly stamping, and a feeble voice from beyond called:

"Nay, wife, there must be something wrong!"

Mistress Whitman opened the door wide and let light into the darkened room.

"Instead, dear husband, 'tis very right," she cried, cheerily, "for here is our precious colt come to visit with you."

True found himself in a small, bare room, standing beside a cot, and, as his eyes grew accustomed to the dimness, he recognized his old master, wasted with illness, lying helpless before him, his cheeks flushed, his eyes bright with fever. The affectionate little horse nosed among the quilts, trying to express his joy at seeing his old friend and at the same time his grief at finding him so weak and ill.

"Wife," called the sick man, presently, "wife, fetch me some maple sugar and do go into the barn and give the colt all there is left of food there."

"I will pay you well, Mistress," said Master Morgan, from the doorway.

"Pay us, sir?" said the feeble voice from the cot, "pay us, sir? For feeding True? Why, bless you, he is one of my own family. I should as soon think of taking pay for food I might give my good wife, there. 'Twas only misfortune that led me to part with our pet. But you mean well, sir, and I bear you no ill-will."

It was thus that True was loved by those who understood his nature.

When at last he was led to the stable he whinneyed twice for Caesar, with leaping heart.

"Was the one from the South who purchased my mother," he asked, "a peerless lily of a maid, with crow-black hair and stars for eyes? Had she palms like the petals of a wild-rose and did she smell like clover blossoms after a sudden shower?"

But Caesar had not noticed, he said, as he sat on the edge of the doorsill, and began his inevitable face-washing.

"Had not noticed! Then indeed, it was not she," thought True, impatient with the cat. Even a *cat* would have noticed Mistress Lloyd.

44

He spent a lonely night and was relieved to set out early in the morning for Randolph, Vermont, where Justin Morgan lived; the old home was not what it had been and any change was better than the atmosphere that hung over all at the Whitman farm.

Besides, Justin Morgan was kind to him and they were good friends enough, and no doubt Randolph was as good a village as Springfield. He grew philosophic as they started off.

They galloped over fields and through vague roads, or walked under vast overhanging and dense forests, and in time they came in sight of the bold, heavily-timbered Green Mountains—"The Footstools of Allah," his mother had called them. They gave the young horse a feeling of strength and confidence; he felt his muscles expand at sight of their bold outlines and he had no fear of their difficulties. From the top of one he gazed at the view, entranced, rearing his fine bony head and breathing deeply of the pure life-giving air.

According to his mother's prophecy it would be in the shadow of these mountains that he, scion of a hundred famous horses, would found the new race, and at first sight of their high broken sky-line, he made a resolve to live such an exemplary life that it would be a standard for that race to come.

Master Morgan was town-clerk, school-teacher, and singing master, and went daily from place to place with books in his saddle bags; it was this life True had come to share. There was a comfortable stable but no stable-mates, and had they not been constantly on the go, True might have been lonely; he came to look for their trips with much content and cantered along right willingly from one place to another.

For a time he was hitched outside the schoolhouse door, but when Master Morgan found he would come at his whistle, he let the little horse graze at will—the bridle fastened securely to the saddle—and to make the acquaintance of other horses during school hours. He knew well True would not abuse this privilege and wander too far.

Thus the first weeks of his stay at Randolph were passed.

As winter set in his sensitive ears detected, high in the air, a snapping of the cold which disturbed him no little, owing to his fear of storms. One night, when this sound was more audible than it had ever been, he pawed and stamped so restlessly that Justin Morgan came to find out what the matter was.

As the stable door opened there flashed through it a flood of crimson light. In the North great shafts pierced from the horizon high into the centre of the heavens. Poor True gave a moan of fright and crowded into a corner of his stall—it looked so like that awful fire in which old Piebald Ceph had lost his life.

Master Morgan closed the door hurriedly.

"Why, you poor horse," he said, kindly, "'tis nothing but the Northern lights. Steady, now, steady."

'Twas not so much the words as the tone and the gentle pats on his shoulder that pacified True. He felt at once that his master would take care of him and calmed himself like a sensible animal.

When he was quieted Justin Morgan climbed into the hay-loft and down a ladder on the other side of the barn rather than let the light shine through the door again, which was very considerate and no doubt True was proportionately grateful.

Those were wild, unsettled days in Vermont, and tales of Indians pillaging and burning were so fresh in the minds of the pioneers that a certain feeling of insecurity remained, ready to be roused into action any minute. The forests were dense and dark, the farms scattered and lonely and the life primitive. Neighbors depended solely upon each other for assistance in times of trouble or danger.

Dame Margery Griswold—daughter of a friendly Indian chief, and wife of a white settler—was one of the fine and noble characters of Randolph. Wise in the ways of medicines and herb-teas, she was constantly called upon to administer to the sick, and never failed to respond, rain or shine, snow or sleet.

One cold, blustery night there came a need for her to go across the mountain to see a child lying sick of a fever.

When she called upon her old white mare she was met by a flat refusal; the poor old nag was crippled with rheumatism and could not rise from her stable floor where she lay on her bedding of dried leaves.

Dame Margery therefore consulted Uncle Peter Edson, to whom all turned for advice, he being the oldest man in the town and a Deacon in the church.

Not long after this Master Morgan was awakened by a smart rapping on his door.

"Who's there?" he called, sleepily.

"Wake, Friend Justin," cried Uncle Peter, for 'twas he. "Dame Margery would borrow your horse Figure for the night. She is sent for to doctor a sick child."

"'Tis a raw night for the dame, no less my horse," answered Morgan, lifting the latch and inviting the old man in out of the cold. The ever-smouldering back-log kept the fire ready to blow into a blaze any time and Justin Morgan, not disturbing his family, set

46

about fanning it with a large, turkey-tail fan. "I do not wish to send my horse out on such a night. We've but just got in ourselves and are fagged," he added.

The fire blazed and was soon roaring up the chimney as the lightwood caught and the pine-knots flamed; then Master Morgan straightened himself.

"By the Constitution of these United States," cried the old man, "'tis not a time to think of brute-beasts. I tell you a *human* lies ill and needs the Dame. Come, come, have done, and let me fetch the horse from the stable!"

But Master Morgan still hesitated, as he hung the turkey-tail back in place beside the high mantel.

"Come, I say," thundered the old man, whom everyone obeyed, "get the horse out, sir, or 'twill be the worse for you when the neighbors find you consider your animal before a human being."

Such threats and language could not be withstood, and Master Morgan, ever willing to be of service to a fellow being, and only reluctant on account of the tired horse, took his lanthorn from the mantel-shelf and went out.

As soon as True left the protection of his stable he felt a storm brewing, not so far away either; he hoped it would not break before his return, yet not knowing where he was going.

Uncle Peter rode him over to Dame Margery's, who, when she came out, was so bundled up in bearskins that had she not spoken at once True might have been startled. Throwing her bags across the saddle and bidding Uncle Peter a cheery good-night she set out on her errand.

It was a cruel night, clouds large and low swept over the moon's face and piled themselves up along the horizon like banks of snow. Dame Margery spoke soothingly and blithely to the horse which partly reconciled him to the dire cold.

When they arrived at their destination Margery went into the hut and a young man came out to throw a fur square over True's shivering back and lead him out of the wind.

Hours passed. Inside the hut a child lay on a pallet on the floor; Margery knelt beside it. Finally she withdrew her arm from beneath the little head very gently and rose to her full, lean height. The white-faced, dry-eyed mother stood near—undemonstrative as Vermont women are apt to be but none the less grateful for all their stillness.

She followed Margery to the door as the latter stepped out into the bitter night.

"Looks like a storm," Margery said, over her shoulder. "See that you don't forget the pleurisy-root tea—and have it piping hot!"

"Best tarry the night," urged the woman, hospitably, from the door where she stood, screening a sputtering dip from the wind with her hand.

"Nay, nay, yet I give you thanks," answered Margery, gaily. "I am not afraid of storms; I was born in one and brought up in a wigwam!"

She pulled the covering from True's back and mounted.

They started just as a veil of blinding snow fell full in their faces—and it fell so fast the ground was soon white.

The vicious wind, like an unchained demon, caught True's thick black mane and blew it upwards, giving him a spasm of cold on his neck. He shivered. A moan swept through the hemlock boughs, they bent before the wind. Margery moistened the end of her finger and held it up, a thin skin of ice formed on its front.

Beaten by the wind and blinded by the snow his old storm-terror came over the horse, he wheeled and let the biting blast beat against his haunches—head down and heavy black tail against the on coming snow and numbing cold.

Once or twice he sniffed, as if in consultation with his rider, but as she offered no advice, he sprang to the shelter of a clump of firs and the harsh wind whistled fiercely on.

Margery slid from the saddle and with stiff but deft hands she caught True's foot and threw him, Indian-fashion, to the ground. Then she broke huge branches of hemlock and piled them up as a brake against the snow, crouching close to the willing body of the now motionless horse. The wind, making a grating sound, pressed hard against their brake but it did not give, and trembling with cold the two waited for the storm to pass. The snow fell and fell; like knives the icy splinters lashed their eyelids and swirled on, tossing wave upon wave of snow on their protection of boughs and mounding it almost over them.

A large branch, heavy with the weight of ice and sleet, snapped from a tree near by and crashed to the ground, but they did not stir.

Angry mutterings came to them through the evergreen branches and shrieked off over the mountains like wind-tossed spirits. Through the long hours they made hardly a movement.

At last the darkness was over and from out the place where it went the sun came, flashing long rays of gold on trees draped with icicles and a world carpeted with snow, sparkling and gleaming, dazzling their eyes with its glitter.

48

A strange calm had fallen on the wind-swept scene when they rose and shook themselves, stiff with cold, to set off homeward. Over all the glistening landscape hung a deep-blue sky, calm, serene.

It was his hardihood that saved the little horse, but good Dame Margery Griswold caught her death that night while the child she braved the storm to save lived on to bless her name.

CHAPTER IX.

TRUE'S FIRST HARD WORK,
AND HOW HE ACCOMPLISHED IT.

Upon a hill at Randolph Centre perched a little store where the farmers gathered in cold weather to warm themselves with Medford rum, a common enough drink in those days, to express lavish opinions as to political affairs of the young nation, so lately separated from her Mother Country, or to discuss more intimate local business.

Master Morgan drank little, being more inclined to quiet study than sociability, but his way led past the store and he often stopped to hear the news. There were no newspapers in those days, and all news came by letter or word-of-mouth of the stage-drivers.

Whilst waiting outside for his owner True made pleasant acquaintances among the horses who also stood awaiting their riders.

A grey mare, very old, very wise and very strong in her convictions, whom he often met, told him many mane-raising stories of Indian days—so recently passed through—and the more his wide-set ears pointed and the more his dark prominent eyes grew eager the better the old pioneer liked it.

One of her strange tales was how she discovered her master, Experience Davis, after he returned from his two years' captivity with the Indians.

One day, she told True, as she stood quietly near Davis' hut, nibbling lazily among the stumps and stones of the new-cleared field to get the last blades of grass and weeds, she heard a frightful sound approaching.

She thrilled with horror!

Davis, hoeing, hard by, also heard and dashed frantically into his hut, closing the door and barring it securely—right well did everyone of the time know what those dreadful war-whoops and blood-curdling yells foreboded!

Old Grey threw back her head and sniffed for a better scent with red, comprehending nostrils. Then, as a band of painted, half-naked savages, brandishing their tomahawks, rushed from the forest, she snorted and fled—her sparse tail high in the air, her heart stricken with fear.

50

On an eminence afar, she stopped and saw the wretches burst open the hut-door and drag her struggling master out. Binding him tightly, and securing everything that might be of use, they set fire to the hut and disappeared into the forest with war-whoops, taking Davis with them.

Old Grey waited sadly on the river-bank until hunger and loneliness induced her to return. Alas, the ruin that met her eyes!

A neighbor who had escaped the massacre of that day found her, wandering about in despair, and, thinking his friend Experience must have been burned in his hut or scalped, took the old mare to share such life as the pioneers of that day had to endure. When he went to live in Hanover, Old Grey went along, too.

One fine sunny day two years later, as she stood hitched in the old Meeting House yard, she felt a thrill, her heart began suddenly to beat faster, she looked around, disturbed in spirit for some strange, unknown reason.

At last she saw a man crossing the yard, and a moment later recognized her old friend Experience Davis!

Fearing he would pass without seeing her, she whinneyed, once-and-a-half, as had been her wont.

Davis stopped, glanced about, mystified, and was going on when she repeated her greeting, anxiously. At that he looked at her, sharply and curiously. Involuntarily he answered, with his old familiar whistle.

At sound of this Old Grey was so overcome with joy that she snapped her hitch-rein with a quick jerk, and trotted right up to him!

He was so pale and thin from long captivity that she would hardly have known him by sight, alone; it was his scent that convinced her infallible nostrils that he was really her once ruddy and strong master.

Davis took her back to the old place where he had just rebuilt the hut and stable and there they had lived happily together ever since.

* * * *

On the Highway from Boston to Canada, stood Benedict's Tavern, and here True often met distinguished horses on their way to or from the race course on The Plains of Abraham, in Quebec, where men sent their horses from great distances to test their speed against other horses. There were then, in the United States of America, no race-courses.

It was at this stage-house, no doubt, that in True was first born that racing spirit, of which nothing came for a long time.

In the late winter of his first year at Randolph, Master Morgan fell ill with lung-trouble; he had to give up his teaching and singing and, finding he could not afford to keep a horse, hired True out to one Robert Evans, a farmer and hunter, solid as granite, and kindly, to clear fifteen acres of heavy-timbered land.

For this task Evans agreed to pay Morgan fifteen dollars and to feed the horse.

Evans, big chinned and grey eyed, was a lean and sinewy frontiersman, poor and hard-working, with a large family, and True knew, intuitively, that his days of pleasant jaunting about the country under the saddle were over. However, with that indomitable courage, which characterizes his descendants to this day, he set about the difficult task and by the first of June it was finished, without help from any other horse.[6]

He never regretted this work for it developed his chest and leg muscles early in life, muscles, the like of which had not been known before in a horse of his size.

The setting of many of True's most interesting experiences and exciting adventures at this period of his life, was Chase's Mill. This busy spot was situated on the wooded bank of the White River, as pretty a bit of Vermont as one could find in a day's journey. The river sparkled and laughed between green banks and leaped merrily over the mill-wheel; spruce and firs thrust thirsty feet deep down in the water and reared tall heads high into the upper air to catch the sun's rays; perfume of wild flowers loaded the breeze; birds sang all day, and white stemmed birches guarded the nearby forest like soldiers standing in a row, straight and firm.

Miller Chase plied an honest trade in Medford rum while the farmers waited for the wobbly stones to grind their corn or the saws to saw their logs. Horses and oxen grazed at hand, taking the opportunity to enjoy the delicious grass growing so abundantly in the rich, fertile valley.

One day True chanced to remark upon this grass to his friend Old Grey.

"Know you not," she asked, astonished at his youthful ignorance, "how it came to be broadcast here?"

"Not I!" whinneyed True. Suffice it that he was enjoying its satisfying plentifulness to the fullest after his hard day in the plow.

And she told him.

After the massacre, in which her master, Experience Davis, had been captured, in plundering Zadock Steele's hut, before burning it, an Indian found a sack of valuable grass-seed. He put it over his shoulder and started off down the valley.

After a while he noticed, vaguely, that his load, unlike the usual manner of loads, became lighter the farther he travelled, but he stupidly did not think to glance over his shoulder at his burden.

When he reached Dog River there was not a grass-seed left in the sack!

Through a tiny hole in the bag he had, unintentionally, sown this wonderful seed all the way from Randolph, and for years it grew up, unmowed, uneaten, and almost man-high, to make the White River Valley famous, and supply grass and hay for farmers and horses.

FOOTNOTES:

[6] *Morgan Horses*, Linsley, page 136.

CHAPTER X.

IN WHICH "TRUE" BECOMES "JUSTIN MORGAN."

Once or twice a week it was the custom among the farmers, waiting at Chase's Mill, to pass the time testing their strength or that of their horses. It was healthful sport and kept them and their beasts in trim.

Many were the jugs of Medford rum consumed on these occasions, and anyone having a horse to try, or a new test of strength for the men, was welcomed.

Running their horses short distances for small stakes came to be very popular.[7] A course of eighty rods was measured, starting at the mill and extending along the highway; a line was drawn across the road, called a "scratch," the horses were ranged in a row, and at the drop of a hat away they went, cheered by the crowd.

It so happened that Evans and True, who never finished their work until dusk, were rarely at these tests. Evans, himself, was too tired to join in the sports, but True often thought he would like to try his strength against the larger, heavier horses.

One day, coming along the River Road to the mill, his heavy farm-harness and tug-chains still dangling on True, they passed Master Justin Morgan—he stood under a maple tree and was lilting an old French song learned from the Canadian lumbermen, called "A la Claire Fontaine." True and Evans paused to listen. Everyone liked Master Morgan for his sweet voice and gentle manners.

When the song was finished Evans gave the singer neighborly greeting and strode on to the mill, True following him, more like a dog than a horse.

The sun was gone and the evening shadows were beginning to fall, but there were still lingering along the horizon long streaks of crimson and gold that tinged the river with color.

In evident discussion, near a log at the mill, stood a group of farmers.

Evans and True approached.

Nathan Nye, friendly and jovial, whittling a birch stick, looked up as Evans said: "How be ye all?"

"Why not give Bob's horse a show?" he asked, a twinkle in his keen blue eyes, a smile brightening his genial face.

Horses and oxen were hitched to the limbs of trees or grazed near at hand, quite without interest in whatever was taking place. Sledges and wagons rested their shafts on the ground, seeming to wait patiently.

"Is it a pulling bee?" asked Evans, leaning against True's side.

"Yaas, but I guess it's abeout over, now," drawled a lank youth, coming out of the mill with a sack of meal on his shoulder.

"Anybody but you in a hurry to be going home-along?" questioned Nye, crushingly.

The youth did not answer, but went on to his sledge.

"There's a jug of Medford rum in the store for the owner of the horse that can get that there log on my runway this evening," explained Miller Chase to Evans.

"Now I want to know!" exclaimed Evans, carelessly, "Why didn't you say so before? You seem to be making quite a chore of a very simple thing; I'll just have my little horse do it for you in a jiffy!"

A shout of derisive laughter greeted his remark.

"Now do tell!" cried Hiram Sage, sarcastically.

"That pony pull a log my Jim refused?" scoffed another.

"My 'pony,' as you call him," laughed Evans, good-naturedly, "has never refused me yet." He placed his arm over True's neck; the horse rattled his chains musically, and reached for a low-handing bough.

"Work is play for this animal," Evans went on. "We've been in the logging-field all day, but that don't make a mite o' difference to the Morgan horse. Come, show us your log!"

True shook himself again and went on chewing leaves.

"Why, that beast's naught but a colt!" said Jim's owner, scornfully.

"Colt or no, he's the finest bit o' horse-flesh this side of The Plains of Abraham!" Evans contended, hotly. "Give him his head and he goes like a shot and doesn't pull an ounce, and as for drawing a load—when this horse starts, *something's* got to come! That is," he added with a laugh, "as long as the tugs last!"

"Well, stop your bragging," said the sarcastic Hiram; "actions speak louder than words. Hitch him up that there 'something' and let us see it 'come'."

Miller Chase stepped forward, hospitably.

"First come in, men, and fix up your bets over a mug," he said.

They went inside the shop, all talking at once, and left True nibbling among the grasses and weeds. When they had disappeared he glanced at the log which the other horses had "refused"—horses much larger and heavier than he. The opportunity he had hoped for had come!

"But can I do it?" he asked himself.

The answer was, he *could*, and *would*.

He was spurred to the greatest effort of his life by the taunt that he was a "pony." At any rate he was over fourteen hands and weighed nine hundred and fifty pounds!

"As I understand it," Evans was saying, as the men came out of the shop, "the agreement is that my horse has got to pull that big log ten rods onto the logway, *in three pulls*, or I lose?"

"That's the idea, exactly," assented Miller Chase.

Evans took hold of True's bridle confidently, and led him to the enormous log, where he fastened the tugs properly. Then he stepped one side and looked the young horse straight in the eye.

True returned his look—they might almost have been said to have exchanged a wink.

At this thought, Evans shouted with laughter.

"Gentlemen," he said, when he could speak seriously, "I am ashamed to ask my horse to pull a little weight like that *on a test*—couldn't two or three of you get on and ride?"

Then Evans was *sure* he saw a twinkle in True's eye.

A loud laugh greeted the proposal.

"But, man, that there's a dead lift!" expostulated the miller.

"Well, mine's a live horse," Evans cried, with a grin. "Get on there! Justin Morgan's waitin' for to take you to drive!"

From this day the young horse was called *Justin Morgan's*. It was an easy transition to drop the possessive "s," after a while, and call him "Justin Morgan."

With much hilarity three men climbed up on the log.

By this time darkness had fallen and Master Chase ran to get his lanthorn, swinging it back and forth, as he returned.

"Mind you don't fall off," Evans warned the men. "'Something' is about to 'come'."

And "something" did!

Justin Morgan's horse gathered himself together, almost crouching, and waited for the word to start. When it was given, his chest-muscles strained, his wide nostrils were scarlet and dilated, and this scion of Arabia's proud breed moved off as if inspired by Allah himself for an almost miraculous feat.

The bystanders, craning their necks to see, ran alongside; the men, perched on the log, fell off as it rocked from side to side, and then the young horse paused for breath—or to recover his strength.

Utter silence was over all. There was no jeering now.

The second pull landed the log on the logway, and the amazed men broke into the wildest cheers ever heard at Chase's Mill.[8]

FOOTNOTES:

[7] *Morgan Horses*, Linsley, page 133.
[8] *Morgan Horses*, Linsley, page 137.

CHAPTER XI.

MORGAN TRIES CONCLUSIONS WITH
THE COXCOMB AND HIS FRIENDS.

After his triumph at Chase's Mill, the Morgan and Evans often stopped there on their way home from work.

A welcome more cordial than usual greeted them one sweet and tranquil afternoon. Cowbells tinkled in the distance, coming home along the River Road for the milking hour, and the chains of Morgan's harness jangled an echo from his sides. The leather parts of this harness were mended here and there with bits of white string, and his usually glossy, short hair was rough and lacked care. He was not pretty, but always bold and fearless in his style of movement.

As was his custom, Nathan Nye sat whittling his birch stick into useless shavings.

"Let the Morgan see if it's *in him to do it*!" he cried to Evans.

"What's the game to-day?" asked Evans, cheerfully.

With a backward nod and a frown Nye indicated three strangers standing in the doorway of the little shop.

"Travellers from over to Benedict's," he explained, in an undertone. "They heard about our horse and have come to try out against him. I've got a sneaking idea that we can take the starch out o' their biled shirts for 'em!" He shut his knife with a determined click and rose. "*They* claim size is necessary for speed and endurance," he went on; "they are just from The Plains of Abraham; on their way back to New York; came yesterday and hearing at the stage-house that we had something of a horse in these parts staid over to-day to satisfy their curiosity."

"We'll satisfy it!" laughed Evans, confidently.

Three strange horses stood hitched near by, and Evans went to take a look at them, as if casually. The Morgan followed, as a faithful dog might, extending his nostrils as he caught sight of a cloak thrown over one of the saddles. He caught the scent and blew his breath on it in a disgusted way. He had recognized the odor of the Coxcomb, Master Knickerbocker!

Nye had also followed Evans.

"I'd just like to show these New York dandies the sort of horses we can raise in Vermont," he said, apparently oblivious of the fact that the best and first part of True's raising had been done in Massachusetts. "Even if we can't afford to use all that ody cologne, and wear frills on our shirt fronts. They say these two horses were bred on the Winooski at the Ethan Allen farm, but this one"—he indicated the horses as he spoke—"is from down New York way."

Evans walked around and looked at them critically.

"Good horses, all of them," he remarked, with appreciation, "and fresh."

"Rested all night at the Inn," Nye corroborated, resentfully.

The Morgan was working himself up over the scent of the cloak—any test for him against the horse on whose saddle it lay was as good as won already. He had an intuition that Mistress Lloyd would like him to defeat the Coxcomb, whose horse was a fretful, vicious animal—handsome enough, it was true, and with many races to his credit—but he was too full of conceit and self-confidence to please Morgan.

The Ethan Allen horses were quieter and gave the impression of reserve power. All three were stylish and well cared for, while Morgan was ungroomed and neglected; there were a few burrs in his heavy black tail, too, which seemed to strike the New Yorkers as extremely amusing. The Morgan, himself, however, had never seen anything very comical about a mere cockle-burr, and was nettled at their foolish remarks and jeers.

"Yes," repeated Nye, "fresh as flowers, and fed to the top-notch. Those men have a fine plan to take us down a peg or two."

"Is it a clean, fair race, think you?" asked Evans, under his breath.

"It's no clean and no fair race," Nye gave reply, indignantly, and in the same low, resentful tone he added,[9] "they want our horse to run three separate races, one after the other, and him all tuckered out with a day's plowing."

"It ain't fair," agreed Evans, vehemently. "My horse ain't only tired, but my saddle and bridle, that I left over here t'other day, ain't light and easy like theirs. It ain't reasonable.... Not but what Morgan can do it," he added, quickly, "but it's hard on him."

"Of course he can do it," assented Nye, confidently. "They say we've got to show 'em—or shut up our bragging over to Benedict's—with the word being passed on from North to South, as never was!"

"All right," said Evans. "We'll show 'em. As long as Morgan's alive we ain't got no cause to shut up bragging."

"Every man to ride his own horse," Nye further explained.

"My legs are a leetle mite too long to be pretty," laughed Evans. "But if Morgan can stand it, I can."

True heard all this as he stood cropping grass near at hand. When they ceased speaking he came and rubbed his nose on Evans' shoulder reassuringly, as he often did in his affectionate, demonstrative way.

At this moment the strangers joined them, and True recognized the Coxcomb as he swaggered forward, tapping his tall boots with a beautiful riding whip. Spurs gleamed on his heels and his insolent manner was in strong contrast to the simple bearing of the straightforward farmer's.

At a glance, Morgan had seen it would be no great feat to beat the Ethan Allen horses, but he also saw with the same quick glance that the New York horse was to be reckoned with; he was evidently accustomed to successes on the course.

When the races were arranged, Evans removed the dangling plow-harness from True's back. At sight of him without it the strangers seemed to be more amused than ever. Their contemptuous remarks affronted Evans.

"Fix up your bets," he called out a moment later, impatiently, seeing how uncomfortable True was with his cumbersome saddle and coarse bit. "I want to get home-along."

He spoke as if he were so sure of winning that it was but the question of a moment or so.

His tone irritated the Coxcomb. He came forward.

"Odd brute that," he sneered, "to put against horses that have won on The Plains of Abraham. But I suppose the *fun* of the races will make up to you for your losses. Why, this is nothing but a Canadian scrub!"

True shook himself in disgust. To be called a striding Canadian. A horse who travels with purposed exertion, while he glided over the ground with scarce an effort. A Canadian scrub, indeed, a horse whose thick nostrils speak of low birth and whose flat sides and thick hair seem made for much cold and beating; and *he*, with the blood of the South in his veins!

It was too much for Evans.

"This is no Canadian," he contradicted, shortly; "this horse is a Thoroughbred."

The Coxcomb laughed derisively, and flicked his boot.

"None the less, the brute would answer to the order '*Marches donc!*'... Not so, my friend?" He struck True on the side with his keen whip, making him spring forward.

"What said I?" he scoffed with a shrug. "The *horse* does not lie about his pedigree."

Ignoring the insulting inference, Evans quieted Morgan with a caress and cried:

"For shame, sir! Would you have me strike *your* horse thus?"

But Master Knickerbocker had moved away, laughing insolently.

The course was measured, the scratch drawn and Nathan Nye stood ready to drop the hat. Several of the men went to the finish-line to witness and testify to the result of the three races.

The course faced the east, so that the eyes of the horses and their riders were turned from the sunset glow which was then illumining the world. The road was smooth, and a recent rain had laid the dust; the conditions were better than usual. The pungent odor of new-sawn lumber filled the air and the chirping of birds from the nearby forest made sweet music.

One of the Ethan Allen horses walked briskly forward under his rider, while the Morgan joined him in the friendly way which was his natural manner towards all animals. They waited pleasantly, yet spiritedly, for the drop of the hat.

When the signal was given they ran neck and neck for a short distance—then with a sudden and unexpected spurt the Morgan dashed in a length ahead.

His friends cheered Morgan lustily; the other faction were too astonished to other than gasp slightly, and were silent. Evans himself was expressionless—if anything, he, as well as Morgan, looked a little bored at the easy victory, and cantered back to the starting point for the next race with a sort of indifference.

The second was twin to the first. Morgan seemed just waking up, as he sprang forward perfunctorily at the finish, winning with ease. He moved as if he knew not fatigue, even after the hard day's work. It was the Desert training of his ancestors within him, their marvellous staying qualities.

When they returned the second time the Coxcomb was waiting, his restive horse trembling in anticipation of a victory.

One or two false starts, and they were off.

The Morgan was away toward the goal like an arrow from an Indian's bow—his small extended muzzle and deep wide chest seemed to cut the air. In the short length of the course he thought of Flying Childers winning his historic race against the runner Fox, about seventy-five years before, of which his father told him. Perhaps this memory and the strain of this great ancestor awakened possibilities within him—the road ran past, his small, well shaped black feet spurned the earth, and before he knew it he was at the finish almost a length ahead of the horse who had won so many races on The Plains of Abraham.

The chagrin of his antagonist's rider was not lessened by the laughs and cheers of the farmers, as they clustered about Morgan and patted his round, deep body and oblique shoulders.

The Coxcomb took his defeat ungracefully and having settled his bets rode impatiently away with his friends.

FOOTNOTES:

[9] *Morgan Horses*, Linsley, page 137.

CHAPTER XII.

OLD GREY TELLS PIONEER TALES.

Many events similar to the one related in the last chapter spread the Morgan's fame throughout the Valley, and when Evans finished his clearing Justin Morgan once more took possession of the horse, for his health was sufficiently restored to take up school-teaching again.

The change from hard farm-work was very agreeable to True, and they cantered from place to place right gaily, albeit the horse missed the sweet singing of Master Morgan, who coughed now incessantly, and often had to dismount and rest in the shade of an oak on the roadside.

He was scarce forty years old, but seemed much more on account of his grievous malady.

Regularly they went to Royalton, some ten miles to the southward, and True grazed about until school let out. Through the window he sometimes saw the gentle, delicate face of the teacher at his desk, his Continental coat slightly open at the throat, showing a bit of fresh white linen, his queue, in the fashion of the day, tied with a stiff bow of black ribband.

He was a master of whom any horse might have been proud.

One day, while waiting for his owner, True wandered into the woods to escape the flies and dust of the highway, and there he met his friend, Old Grey, who told him how the Indians had burned Royalton in 1780; and among the anecdotes relating to this time there was one which amused the young horse no little.

It ran as follows:

For some unaccountable reason the Indians had failed to burn the hut of one Jones, who had a wife known far and wide as a scold and a shrew. To get a day's rest from her abuse, poor Jones oft-times had to go hunting or trapping, and when he saw an especially bad tantrum coming he would snatch his gun from the mantel-shelf and, calling his dog, rush forth into the forest, a storm of reviling in his wake. Sometimes he remained away for days.

Nobody ever remembered having seen Jones smile.

One day, his wife's temper and tongue being worse than usual, he found it expedient to go hunting, and stayed away over night. There are times when a silent dog is sweet company and the peaceful forest a haven of refuge.

On the second afternoon, thinking it might be safe to return, Jones approached his home cautiously. Stranger sounds than usual greeted his listening ear.

He paused, alert and intent, silencing his intelligent dog with a gesture. Creeping stealthily forward under the shadow of the trees, he beheld a small band of Indians in the act of breaking open his hut-door. He waited tensely, to see them drag his wife out and scalp her.

Instead, from inside came her familiar voice raised in vitupera-tion and upbraiding. Jones could scarcely believe his ears, and for the first time since his marriage he grinned.

"This time those red imps have met their match," he murmured to his dog with an audible chuckle.

Hardly had he spoken when out came half a dozen Indians drag-ging the shrew between them. Not for one moment, however, did she cease her abuse, terrified though she surely must have been.

Jones, standing at the edge of the forest, watched—fearfully at first, then with curious interest. Finally he sat down on the ground and gave way to uncontrollable mirth.

The Indians had paused on the river bank in consultation.

Suddenly, without warning apparently, two of them gathered the scold in their arms and sprang into the chill water. The others stood on the bank and whooped mad encouragement, fiendishly, as only Indians can.

Mistress Jones' green homespun petticoat filled quickly with air and swelled around her like an enormous squash, out of which her scarlet face glowed furiously.

The savages on the bank yelled and danced. Those in the water ducked their victim up and down, howling with glee, cracking her over the head as she rose.

"And there be some who say an Indian can't see a joke," splut-tered Jones, under his breath, holding his sides. The dog looked at his master with suspicion—he thought the man was choking.

But Jones soon saw that the savages merely meant to discipline his wife and give her a bath. An interruption from him might disturb these laudable intentions, so he remained quietly in the background.

When they had finished to their entire satisfaction they lifted the woman out of the river and flung her, gasping and shivering, among the tree-roots on the bank. She looked like a huge wet log. Yelling, they swam the river and disappeared in the dense woods beyond.

Trembling, Jones drew near—his mirth turned to seemly gravity; but he found a very subdued person. Cautiously Mistress Jones opened her eyes, one at a time, first peering carefully between the lids to see if the approaching footsteps were those of her tormenters returning.

When she saw her husband she groaned feebly.

"Have they gone?" she whispered.

"Yes," replied Jones, with becoming seriousness.

Mistress Jones rose heavily, and squeezed the water from her skirts, shaking, humble and sobered.

"It served me right, husband dear," she wailed at last. "I have ever been what those savages called me, 'a dirty blouze of a thing,' but from now on I am a changed woman and will be a better wife to you. The Indians said they would teach me a lesson—and they have!"

CHAPTER XIII.

THE MORGAN GOES TO MONTPELIER TO LIVE.

Sometimes Justin Morgan rode his horse to Williston to visit his friend, the Hon. Lemuel Bottom, who was a lover of good horses; sometimes they went to Hinesburgh, a short distance from Burlington. They were constantly on the go from one town to another, meeting new people and horses and having fresh experiences.

Hinesburgh was a quiet little village, and, although there were two saw-mills, they did not have "bees" as they did at Randolph; the scenery was beautiful, and the bedding so good that Morgan enjoyed his trips in spite of the lack of excitement which he had grown to love at Chase's Mill.

His first military experience was when he took his place under an empty saddle in the procession that conducted the body of Col. Israel Converse to his grave. Colonel Converse had been a brave soldier and greatly beloved by his townspeople; over his open grave Morgan heard for the first time a military salute and smelled the acrid odor of gunpowder. For a long time he was thrilled by the memory.

As time increased Master Morgan's health declined rapidly; in 1795-96 he grew too weak to work, and sold his horse to one William Rice, of Woodstock, who in turn sold him to Jonathan Shepard, a sturdy blacksmith living in the little town of Montpelier.

Shepard was also landlord of the Farmer's Inn, which stood within a doughnut's toss of his forge. He was an energetic, thrifty man, and Colonel Davis engaged him to do some clearing on his farm, seeing that he now had a good strong young horse. Thus Morgan once more became a farm-horse, but as Shepard was well to do and kind, he fared well in his new home.

His dinner in a pail, and oats in a sack for the Morgan, Shepard would go out for a day's plowing or clearing the while Mistress Shepard remained at home to serve customers at the Inn.

A "halloo" from the forge would make the blacksmith hurry back to aid a passing traveller whose horse had cast a shoe or whose wagon or "shay" needed mending. He would leave the Morgan in the care of Maximus Fabius Davis, the son of Colonel Davis, who—as boys went, in Morgan's estimation—was pleasant enough. Mor-

66

gan was ever fond of men and women, already grown, but the stage of childhood, required to develop them into such, did not seem to interest him.

Now and again Maxy would ride him home in the evening, and if there chanced to be a horse at the forge anxious for a test, there would be a race or some trial at pulling. Tales of his speed and strength spread for miles around, and all who called at the Inn or the forge were anxious to see him. But they always said afterward it was a shame to turn such a fine animal into a mere farm-horse. Shepard had his answer ready, that he "was but a farmer himself, and needed a good plow-horse—not a racer eating its head off in his stable."

Through honesty and that thrift for which the Vermonter is famous Shepard soon acquired considerable wealth, and wanting a larger place he exchanged the Morgan, his smithy, and the Farmers' Inn for the large farm on Dog River, belonging to James Hawkins. Thus, Morgan changed owners, but not homes, for Hawkins came to Montpelier to live. The horse was glad of this, for he liked the musical ring of the hammer on the anvil and the glare of the forge as the handle of the bellows was raised and lowered.

Montpelier, organized in 1793, was a village of little consequence, but one of its citizens was a man of parts, staunch and true, and destined to rise to the high position of Secretary of State. His name was David Wing, Jr., and he often borrowed the Morgan from Hawkins for as much as a week at a time. Under the comfortable saddle of Master Wing, Morgan first saw the beautiful Winooski, with its sweep of eddies and currents, its foaming rapids and singing falls. David loved nature and good scenery as much as Morgan and their trips were sweet and pleasant through lovely, fertile valleys and across densely wooded hills; along frequented highways or vague trails through the forests.

Sometimes they went as far as Burlington and Morgan had to cross many streams and wade through foaming, circling water, which, when very deep, gave him a sense of adventure. He was always ready to swim if the need came, and would have hesitated at nothing his rider set him to do, such confidence did he feel in Man-wisdom.

If they were not in a hurry David would allow him to play along the way, knowing well enough the horse would not abuse the privilege. He rode with a loose rein, and on the way home would let the Morgan choose his own gait and trail. The firm touch on the bridle was as light as a woman's, but Morgan was not fooled by it. He well knew this was a rider who would brook no impertinence, and it kept him steady and respectful, even while he took advantage of the permission to frolic a little.

These two saw many strange sights in their wanderings—sights that later history proved were the making of a fine and sturdy race of men and horses.

Ofttimes, in bitter winter weather, they passed little bare-foot children on their way to school, carrying their shoes in their cold hands, to put on, in a very elegant manner, at the school-house door; to *walk* in them would have been *wilful extravagance*, though their toes were blue with cold! If, by chance, they found a cow lying down, chewing on her morning cud, they would disturb her rudely and make her get up, that they might put their bare feet on the spot she had so nicely warmed for her own comfort.

But better and more prosperous times were coming, and it was not long before shoes were looked upon as a necessity for children, not an extravagance, though they were ever evil-smelling things— the leather being home-tanned and home-cured and needing much greasing at night to keep it soft enough to make the shoes wearable. They made an unseemly clumping on the floor, and were very ugly, but their aim being use, not beauty, this was no drawback.

* * * *

Sometimes kind and gentle Mistress Hannah Wing rode the Morgan to a quilting bee, or meeting, or to such entertainments as ladies saw fit to attend. She was good to him and made his visits to their barn most pleasant. In the mornings she would come tripping out, her arms full of dew-wet clover or grass, just cut, or she would have a dish of goodies from the kitchen—some carrots or turnips. 'Twas no wonder the horse loved her and called to her, as she drew near, with his affectionate little neigh. He always hoped David might buy him from Hawkins; he loved the Wings and they returned his friendship. And a horse never knows when he may change owners. He can only hope his next one may be the one of his choosing, which does sometimes happen.

The minds of the Vermonters in those days dwelt on higher things than fashions, especially with the men, and the wearing of beavers was not common, unless perhaps the hat was inherited. Hats were so much better made then, and so expensive, that a beaver lasted from thirty to forty years, and was passed on from father to son. In this way it had come to be looked on as frivolous and extravagant to be seen in a new one; if any man had the courage to buy such, he left it out in the weather a few nights to *"take that new look off"* before he wore it in public.

At this time David Wing was town-clerk, and one day on his return from a trip to Boston, by stage, he brought home something in what was unmistakably a hatbox.

Gossip concerning so important a man soon flew about, and the box became town-talk before the day was over. Women folks came, on one pretext or another, to call on Mistress Wing. Some asked her rule for wheaten cake, others how she made her cheeses, and so on. But it did not take their clever hostess long to find out the true aim of their calls, and being right proud of the hat herself, she took it out of the box and showed it to them all. 'Twas very tall and glossy, and shaped liked the rain barrel; the brim was so low in front it would hide its wearer's nose completely; suddenly it curved sharply at the sides in the manner of a drawn bow; and, all told, it was an elegant bit of the latest Boston fashion.

'Twas to be worn, Mistress Wing informed her callers, for the first time at meeting the next Sabbath.

Many were the exclamations of "Land sakes!" and "Do tells!" that the sight of the hat provoked, and much pleased was Mistress Hannah to be able to awaken so much admiration for her husband's taste.

Unfortunately David did not wait until the Sabbath to wear his new hat; had he done so history, in all likelihood, would never have recorded the fact that he had owned a beaver.

The very next morning he came swinging out of the house looking most gentlemanly in his high stock, ruffled shirt and shining boots. On his head sat, most jauntily, the new hat.

David was off for a town meeting.

Down the road cantered Morgan, meeting many acquaintances who paused in speechless admiration until they passed out of sight. Some with envy, alack; some with criticism of the extravagance, but others with friendly nod of greeting and approval.

The sun shone, the crisp air was fragrant with pine needles, and birds chirped in the trees that fringed the highway. Morgan champed his bit and curvetted from one side of the road to the other, his heart full of the morning freshness.

Suddenly a yellow dog came in sight, and the horse, full of fun and spirit, lowered his head and made a dash at him, remembering his colt-days and the game of "Red-Coats." The dog tucked his tail between his hind legs and made off down the road at lightning speed.

This was enough to rouse Morgan; even though he did not like dogs, he thought it might be a race. Helter, skelter, he started; ever fleet in running, he was soon gaining slowly, but surely, on the dog, who was little more than a yellowish brown streak on the landscape.

Morgan heard David say, good-naturedly:

"Go it, my boy, stop when you get good and ready; I am having as much fun as you."

Once, as the dog glanced hurriedly back over his shoulder, the horse saw his tongue hanging out—he looked almost winded, but his pace was long and even, like Morgan's, and his flapping ears responded rhythmically to his gait.

Morgan tossed his head and made a movement with his tail as much as to indicate he had just begun to race. The rapid clatter of his own hoofs on the hard road was music to him.

Seconds passed. Then the dog disappeared at a sharp bend in the road.

Losing sight of him for a moment nerved Morgan to a sudden spurt. With all his power impelling him he, too, rounded the corner—and ran headlong into two horsemen who had been jogging peacefully and unsuspectingly along the quiet and seemingly deserted highway.

What a reckoning there was! Never was such confusion! Lawyer Buckley slid from the back of his pony and his books broke from the strap and were scattered over the road; Dr. Pierce's saddle bags burst open and pills and bandages fell out as if to offer their help in the emergency.

Morgan, realizing he had caused all the trouble, kept his presence of mind admirably, and stood firm and motionless where his front feet had plowed into the earth at his sudden halt. David did not lose his seat, but the stop, without any warning, almost threw him over Morgan's head.

When things had steadied a bit, and explanations and apologies made, David noticed for the first time, as he put his hand up to remove his hat, and wipe the perspiration from his brow, that his beaver was missing.

Under the very feet of Dr. Pierce's nag, who stood still snorting her expostulations, it was found. Lawyer Buckley picked it up, shaking his head with ill-concealed satisfaction.

"'Tis but a crushed and torn rag," he said, brushing it the wrong way with the sleeve of his coat; "but you have that young Morgan to thank for the prank."

At these words Morgan was more mortified than ever, though he could not help glancing furtively about for the dog and pricking his ears back and forth for sounds. Soon he espied and heard him a short way ahead, yelping from the cover of his owner's hut, surrounded by a protecting and gaping crowd of small bare-foot children who had assembled from the other side of the house to find out what the matter was.

It is not necessary to relate with what fallen crest Morgan bore his rider home after the day closed in. The hat, so lately the envy of the whole town, hidden under his rider's coat, to be laid away until Mistress Hannah could restore it to some of its first magnificence.

CHAPTER XIV.

MORGAN MAKES A TRIP TO BOSTON.

For several days Morgan showed his regret at the fate of the beaver by neither romping nor playing. When David and himself were on their way from place to place and resting at noon, he cropped grass in a very staid and dignified manner, whilst David sat in the shade and ate his luncheon of light wheaten cakes and cheese, the two things for which Mistress Hannah was famous.

On these trips they sometimes met the Boston-Canada stage coaches, carrying the mail, and they would stand one side and watch the horses running at full speed over the rough roads; the horn winding a lusty warning to private coach, curricle or rider, that might be approaching from the other direction round a sharp bend in the way.

Again they would pass lazy oxen, drawing their sleds slowly to market, or coming home from mill, their loads creaking behind them as they swayed awkwardly from side to side, responding reluctantly to the goad-sticks in their drivers' hands.

These pioneer teams drew the products of the outlying farms—maple sugar, and potash and "black salts"—(gathered by thrifty farmers from the ashes of winter fires or logging heaps)—to the towns.

The forests of Vermont at first were gloomy and almost impenetrable, tending, some claimed, to make the people grave and serious, but already the lumber industry had begun the destruction of the beautiful woods of hemlock, birch, white pine, ash, chestnut and stately oak. Saw-mills whirred and sang busily on river banks, whose falls afforded such marvellous water-power for their wheels, and comfortable houses soon took the place of pioneer huts in many places.

In spite of his faithful service to the Wings, they did not buy the Morgan, and Hawkins after a while sold him to the same Robert Evans, at Randolph, for whom he had once done such good service.

Randolph had a newspaper now, called *The Weekly Wanderer*, and this praised the Morgan so highly that for a while, out of pride, Evans had to keep him in good condition. But unfortunately this pride lasted but a short time, Evans being too busy at his farm work and trapping, earning a living for his family.

On the day of his return to Randolph, Morgan heard that Master Justin Morgan had gone on to "lie in green pastures, beside still waters." So sweet a sound had this to the lonely horse, separated from his good friends in Montpelier, that he sometimes wandered away from the Evans' primitive barn, looking for that "Valley of the Shadow" of which men spoke when referring to the kindly school-master. The heat of the mid-summer days sometimes oppressed the little horse, and he grew thin and weary at the plow, but there was no "Valley of the Shadow" for him—no other valley could he find than his work-a-day one along the banks of the sparkling White River in full sunshine.

In the weary battling against the uncongenial farm life, he was no little cheered by the memory of what his father told him of his high-crested ancestor, the Godolphin Arabian—that he, in all his greatness and beauty, had once pulled a water cart in France.

In a year the brave little horse was unrecognizable; his once glossy, soft coat had coarsened, and often he was humiliated by the knowledge that there were burrs in his tail and in the bit of dark hair that grew above his fetlocks.

Chase's Mill was still the centre of the town's gaiety; occasionally there were races, but rarely were the horses worth Morgan's effort.

In spring, when the world was full of flowers, and orchids and blue flags hung their banners out to tempt the Evans children into the woods, Morgan would go with them to gather these or the more useful medicinal herbs for times of sickness—pleurisy-root, marsh-mallow or ginseng. In summer he went with them to pick berries of all sorts or wild grapes, and when the autumn came, with its glory of beech and maple, turning to copper and scarlet, he would bring home their bags of nuts across his round back.

In winter his coat grew long and thick; and Evans himself rode him to distant traps set in the forest for bear, musk-rat and foxes, which supplied food or clothing for the family. The horse grew accustomed after a while to the monotony of his life and tried to make the best of it.

One cold, clear day Evans cleaned him so very carefully Morgan felt sure something was about to happen, but did not try to guess what; he had learned the futility of that long ago, for things never came about as he guessed or planned they should.

In the course of time, however, he found himself cantering along the stage-road to Boston. It was a trip he had long wanted to take, so

73

many horses had told him what a beautiful and gay city it was.

The day being severely cold, he was glad enough of the long legs and homespun woolen breeches of his rider which covered so much of his sides. As for Evans, he had his muskrat cap pulled well over his ears and his home-made boots of calf-skin (smelling horribly of grease), with the heavy breeches tucked well inside, were warm and comfortable to his feet.

But they must have cut a sorry figure when they reached Boston and went along Summer Street; that lovely, fashionable thorough-fare, with its stately trees, beautiful flower gardens and splendid mansions.

It was dusk when they stopped in Corn Court, at the Braser Inn—the famous hostelry opened by Samuel Cole, in 1634, where Miantonomah's painted Indians—envoys to Sir Harry Vane—had been entertained; where the French Premier, Talleyrand, had so late-ly stayed; where so many other events of history had taken place.

As Evans was hitching his horse to a post near the side door of the tavern, Morgan heard a familiar, bantering voice; the odor of musk came to his nostrils faintly, and glancing about, he saw—as he knew he should—the Coxcomb.

No fop of the King's court could have looked more elegant; his Continental coat, cocked hat and high shining boots were of the lat-est cut—not less offensive to the simple taste of the horse was his insolent swagger.

Master Knickerbocker, of course, did not notice Morgan, but cried to Evans persuadingly:

"Tarry the night, my Green Mountain Giant, we can show you rare sport at cards if you've money in your purse."

Evans towered above the popinjay as his Green Mountains would have towered over Beacon Hill. He gazed down at him with contempt, vaguely, yet not definitely, recognizing his one-time an-tagonist in a race, as Morgan had.

"I have no money to lose to you, my young sir," he made reply, ungraciously. "I am but a simple farmer, and I play with none but my own kind. I do not know the rules by which such as you handle the cards!"

"Then join us in a glass of Medford rum—such as you Vermon-ters know so well how to appreciate—'tis cold outside and the land-lord will mull us a bowl. Come, I say!"

He clapped the farmer hospitably on the shoulder in friendly fashion, and led the way into the tavern.

A kind bar-maid came out and threw a fur square over Morgan's shivering back and give him a warm mash, which comforted him greatly. He acknowledged her friendliness, by nipping her sleeve gently with his lip; and as she was fond of horses, this pleased her, and she further brought him joy by patting his face gently and murmuring little love-talk in his ears.

Many hours later the side door opened and the Coxcomb came out. He was talking to himself as he closed the door behind him, blotting out the sudden radiance from the great, roaring fire inside the tavern. He did not notice Morgan, though he almost touched him in the darkness as he paced to and fro.

"Egad!" he cried, under his breath; "the fellow had money—but he has it not. Let him go back where he belongs, to his land of hemlock and frost-bitten, half-civilized race.... Yet," and he almost sighed—not quite, "even *I* awakened to a slight feeling of compunction when he turned out the toe of a woman's stocking and confessed it was his last shilling—money, he remembered too late, his wife had given him to buy a calico gown.... Ha! Calico, at the trifle of three shillings the yard! Mistress Lloyd"—here Morgan pricked his ears back and forth—"Mistress Lloyd wears silks and satins, and her laces are like cobwebs.... Oddsbodikins! *There* is a maid to turn a man's head—even mine! 'Twill not be long now before my suit prospers.... I have won everything from her father but his daughter, and I shall bide my time till I win her. I have made up my mind—I, and not Dulaney, will live 'Where the Great Lloyd sets his Hall!'"

Almost under Morgan's nose he drew from his satin waistcoat-pocket a snuff-box wrought in gold by a master craftsman. With the tips of his delicate fingers he daintily pinched a few grains of the evil-smelling powder and placed it to his nostrils.

Morgan sneezed.

The Coxcomb stepped hurriedly aside with a prodigious oath as the door of the Inn swung open.

Robert Evans stalked out into the night, his cap pulled over his ears, his fur cape wrapped tight about his shoulders. The Coxcomb greeted him with a condescending smile and extended his snuff-box.

The giant waved it aside with a gesture of dignity and scorn.

"No, sir," he said, shortly; "if the good Lord had intended my nose for a dirt-box, he would have put it on upside down!"

Master Knickerbocker laughed, though Evans had not intended to be funny.

"Egad! A very good sally!" he drawled. "Yet I but tried to show my friendliness."

"'Tis a pity you had not tried to show it earlier in the evening," returned Evans, gruffly, as he mounted his horse and rode away.

Good Dame Evans would have no calico gown from Boston, that was sure, and 'twas money she'd saved for years from her cheese and butter sales, and kept in an old bee-hive in the attic, saying no word to anyone of it.

Now her sacrifices had gone to purchase snuff and perfume for the Coxcomb.

Morgan had often seen Dame Evans give the traditional Vermont "beech seal" to her sons—and he would not deny they needed it; and he had seen her dash scalding water on a prowling Indian; he guessed Robert Evans' greeting, when they reached home, would not be an affectionate one.

On the way back to Randolph, Evans was in a temper and swore grievously. Morgan had caught a cold and coughed constantly. The journey was withal a trying one; 'twas not to be wondered at that the horse's memories of Boston were neither beautiful nor gay, and that he never had a desire to repeat his trip.

It was dark when they reached home, but Mistress Evans, who had been on the lookout, threw open the kitchen door as they entered the gate, and the barnyard was flooded with the warm glow of the firelight from within. Her head was tied up in a fustian square and a fur was thrown over her shoulders. She ran out to greet them, a lanthorn in her hand.

"Welcome, home, Husband, dear!" she cried, cheerily. "Give me the purchases. I would see my calico frock without delay. Yes, and get to work on it, for 'tis no short task to stitch those long seams—with chores to do besides!"

She held out her hand eagerly.

"Go into the house directly, Wife, out of the cold!" evaded Evans, taking the lanthorn from her. "I will be in presently—when I have bedded down the Morgan," he added.

And she, being an obedient, womanly and faithful wife, suspecting nothing, went in to sing over the final preparations of supper.

In spite of the cold and fatigue of his owner, Morgan never got a better rubbing-down nor a finer meal.

"Well, Morgan," Evans murmured, at last, "I guess I can't put it off any longer."

He dragged his reluctant feet slowly toward the house, where Dame Evans was waiting for him with steaming hulled corn, fried pork and maybe something else—when she found out his secret!

CHAPTER XV.

FOR MISTRESS LLOYD, OF MARYLAND.

In 1803 Morgan went to pass a week with his old friends, the Wings, and the visit was one long to be remembered.

The talk of the village was Mistress Hannah's new silken gown—the first ever brought to Montpelier, so the town history tells. David Wing was now Judge and Secretary of State, and his wife had to wear fine clothes, as befitted her station, for many were the calls on her to entertain distinguished guests.

It was at a meeting in their new barn that Mistress Wing first wore the wonderful silk. All the other ladies present had on home-spun and linen—silk would have been called "flunk and flummux" on them.

The Judge that day wore his Indian cotton shirt with the frills—hemmed and tucked. It made a brave show, for cotton was three shillings the yard at that time.

I mention these historic facts merely to show that Morgan played his part with the Quality of the times, as well as at the plow, and to occupy a stall in the Judge's grand new barn was no small privilege to a horse!

But the greatest pleasure of all was when he heard that Colonel Lloyd of Maryland, and his daughter had come a'visiting the Judge and his lady.

The Wings and the Lloyds had met in New York the winter before and the Judge had unwoven some legal tangles for the Colonel. A friendship had resulted and now the Southerners had come all the way from Maryland in their coach to enjoy the cool, summer breezes of Vermont under the hospitable roof of their New England friends.

When the Judge brought them out to see his new barn Morgan recognized the swish of her petticoats at once, as Mistress Lloyd drew near the stable.

Knowing how they loved good horses their host threw open Morgan's door.

There was an instant's pause, then:

"Why, I *know* this horse!" cried Mistress Lloyd. "*I* gave him his first blue ribband!"

Oh, the melody of her voice, and the feel of her cheek against his! At last, after years of parting, they met—and she had not forgotten him. Oh, wondrous memory of such a woman as she!

Morgan was glad the Judge's hired man had groomed him so carefully that morning, and that not long before, the stable floor had been strewn with fresh, sweet sawdust.

"What a noble animal you've grown to be!" she whispered in his waiting ear. "I predicted it full ten years agone!"

So it had been ten years since he had seen her last, yet he had cherished her, and she him, in memory, all that long time of busy scenes apart.

He pushed his small muzzle in and out among the laces and gauzes of her neck so gently they were not disarranged, and she pressed her cheek close to his. Something in the tones of her voice told him she was not happy, and as the delicious odor of her hair entered his nostrils he whinneyed a question, softly.

As if understanding, she answered, murmuring near his ear,

"Dear Little Horse," there was a catch in her voice, "I cannot buy you, even now, for our money is all gone! Daddy is no manager; he has ever been what they call a 'gentleman' and our family mansion—'where the Great Lloyd sets his Hall'—is to be sold to pay a most unjust 'debt of honor'—I call it a debt of *dis*honor, for 'twas made at the gaming table; and though Judge Wing be ever so clever, he can do nothing now for my father and me!"

She leaned against Morgan; he heard a sob in her throat as she clasped his arched neck.

He whinneyed his tenderest sympathy, and maybe she would have told him more, but there came a sound of voices through the open door.

"Ah, here you are, my daughter!" It was the Colonel speaking. "Come and greet our friend who has ridden all the way from Boston to see us. He says he has a plan whereby we may save our home!" Colonel Lloyd spoke hopefully, if a little doubtfully.

Mistress Lloyd turned her face, flushed with emotion, and saw the Coxcomb, of whom Morgan had just caught scent.

"A plan?" she questioned him, after a cold greeting. "You mean a price! 'Tis the same old one," she said wearily, "I do not need to be told!"

"My price," he answered, shrugging his shoulders, "is offered out of friendship for your father and—"

"You need not say!" she interrupted him, contemptuously. "'Tis not for *friendship* you do kindnesses!"

"You know my price," he said, with calm insolence. "I have waited long," he added, under his breath.

"I will never pay it!" she replied with steady scorn, but so firmly Master Knickerbocker could not but believe her.

The truth was, he wanted her to be his wife, and she, knowing what manner of man he was, had withstood his importunities for years. She would none of him.

She held her head high.

He shrugged his shoulders and raised his eyebrows.

"As you will, Mistress! In one week more you and your father will be beggars, and living on the charity of your friends—unless?" He flicked his riding boot with his whip and looked at her with defiance.

There was a short silence during which the lady grew very haughty, and then began to move away.

"Come," the Coxcomb spoke again, in a different tone, following after her. "You love a good race—you're a Southerner—what say you to a *race—yourself and your home* the stake? If you win I will cancel all these notes I hold against your father and accept your refusal to marry me as final. If I win, ah——"

Mistress Lloyd silenced him with a movement; she was no longer the slip of a girl True knew at Hartford. Here was a mature character of spirit and dignity, yet not lacking in the sweetness of perfect womanhood.

"I understand—you need not put the rest in words. I will *ride* your race, *on this very horse*—and you?"

"I have Silvertail with me," he answered, and in an undertone added, "You will not have the ghost of a chance!"

If Mistress Lloyd did not hear this, Morgan did, and switched his tail with satisfaction, moving his ears to and fro, to miss nothing.

Silvertail! If horses could laugh aloud, Morgan would have laughed. He recalled a race six years before against Silvertail and it seemed almost a miracle that he should meet him again—of all the other horses in America—in so important an event.

"I am not afraid of Silvertail," came Mistress Lloyd's brave reply.

The Coxcomb looked at Morgan scornfully, not remembering how he, too, had been defeated by him years ago, at Chase's Mill!

"Then 'tis settled," he said, confidently.

"Nay, not settled!" cried the lady, with well-feigned gaiety. "We've yet to put the matter in writing, all in due form with the Judge to advise." For Mistress Lloyd was no careless person, when it came to business, nor no mean reader of men.

She placed her hand for a moment under Morgan's jaw and felt his pulses surge in response to her touch; then she drew herself erect, reassured—as if the race were already won!

They left the stable making their plans.

An hour later, Judge Wing and the Colonel came into the Morgan's stall.

"My dear sir," the Colonel was saying, "the folly of it! My daughter—and to ride for such a stake! But you know the girl. She has set her heart on it—I can do nothing. She winds me about her finger as if I were a piece of string, since her dear mother died. Our trouble is all my fault, what with mortgages and debts of honor, I am well paid for my follies—and, after all, this race is better than seeing her married to the author of all our unhappiness. Yet if she should not win!"

"No need to worry over that, my friend," the Judge said. "Morgan has already beaten this Silvertail horse."

"You don't tell me!"

"I recall the circumstances perfectly," continued the Judge. "Silvertail[10] is a horse with a reputation; he was bred in St. Lawrence County, New York, and the Morgan once won a stake of fifty dollars in a race against him. It was in the life-time of Justin Morgan himself, and Master Morgan, sir, offered Silvertail two chances to redeem himself afterwards, in either walking or running, but the offer was declined. The world doesn't know Morgan, but I do, and our race is already won!"

The horse arched his crest at these words of praise.

"Then all is said!" cried the Colonel, in a tone of relief. "My daughter is the finest horse-woman in Maryland, and that is no mean praise."

He came to Morgan and placed his hand lightly on the horse's broad forehead, and seeing the Judge had turned away, spoke softly near the pricking ear.

"Save her, Little Horse, and I will never touch another card!"

Already Morgan could feel the finish of that race and see the flaxen-maned Silvertail toiling behind. He had little regard for a horse with light points (but which do well enough for mere beauty); deep in his heart his respect was for dark points, at once indicating possibilities of strength, docility and endurance—he had *proven* these qualities and knew!

That afternoon, the sun still high, he was led out to be exercised and prepared for the race.

Then She came, and, mounting him, rode easily and gaily down the stretch of road to the blacksmith shop where the course, as usual, was marked out along the highway.

In the fashion of the day her purple habit almost swept the ground as she sat her saddle with firm confidence; her wide hat and plume falling to her shoulders, framed her high-bred face. Her eyes sparkled—for the moment she almost seemed to have forgotten the nature of the stake! Hers was the embodiment of that Southern spirit of which Beautiful Bay had so often told True.

Her grasp of the bridle rein was as gentle as a caress, but as firm as steel—showing, well, she would brook no foolishness from a horse.

Against the sky the Green Mountains reared their heads, the pastureland on their sloping sides was patched here and there with cloud-shadows, and, where the sun's rays slanted on the Winooski it glittered like a silver line in the valley. No wind, and a late rain, made the condition of the road perfect.

Loitering about the smithy were a few men who roused themselves at sight of the Morgan cantering up with a lady on his back.

Across the way, on the Inn porch, the sound of voices rose and fell in argument over the policies of Thomas Jefferson, the "Farmer" President; the purchase of Louisiana from the French, and such topics of the time. The idle men to whom the voices belonged sat in a row, their chairs tilted against the wall, but when they saw the Coxcomb swagger forth, they brought them down to the floor, simultaneously, and stared curiously.

Silvertail was led up and the slender New Yorker swung himself lightly into the saddle.

The idlers rose, gazed after the retreating horseman a moment, then strode with one accord down the Inn steps and on to the smithy, just in time to see the Coxcomb give Mistress Lloyd a grand sweep of his hat, as he said gallantly:

"'Tis hard to beat so fair an antagonist, but the stake is one I must win!"

"The race is yet to be run!" the lady made reply, smiling, securely.

She released the fastenings of her plumed hat and tossed it to her father.

"Catch, Daddy, dear! I ride with no frills and furbelows to-day! I wish I were that light Francis Buckle. Do you recall, Father, how he won last year at Epsom on Tyrant, the very worst horse that ever won a Derby?"

"My daughter is almost as light as Buckle and the Morgan a better horse. We have nothing to fear!" So spoke Colonel Lloyd, bravely, and, patting Morgan's long shoulder, he raised his hat with courtly grace and bade his daughter, "God-speed!" right gaily.

And Mistress Lloyd? She laughed serenely—that same brook-like laugh of long ago; her lip did not quiver nor her voice tremble. With such spirit do men go into battle. She gathered the reins in her slim, bare hands—no gloves should come between her and Morgan's mouth that day—and smiled at her antagonist, as if to say:

"Morgan and I do not fear you and Silvertail!"

When Silvertail recognized Morgan, which he did at once, he began to fret and prance. Morgan, however, made no false motions; he was saving every fibre of energy. With eager nostrils and arching crest he waited the signal to start.

The Coxcomb sat his horse with consummate grace, but his eyes glittered cruelly, in a way that boded ill for Silvertail. In his hand he carried a silver-mounted whip, on his heels spurs shone.

Mistress Lloyd, on the other hand, had neither whip nor spur; she ever depended on the tones of her voice for success with horses; sitting like a model for an Amazon, she waited, calm, serene.

A furtive backward glance from Silvertail's eye said plainly enough, "For less than a carrot I'd bolt, to get out of this race!"

Once Morgan quivered as he remembered what his father had told him of Eclipse: "Eclipse first, the rest nowhere!"

To-day it should be "Morgan first, Silvertail nowhere!" The breeze blew lightly at his mane, his eyes glowed, his neck strained as the signal was given.

Morgan leaped forward. They were off!

Swift, as one of a race divine who flies, rather than treads the earth, Morgan's deep, wide chest cleaved the air.

Pressing close came Silvertail, breathing heavily.

Mistress Lloyd had given Morgan his head, with intimate trust and understanding. He would win—in his own way—and she knew it. She was low in the saddle, leaning close to his extended neck, pressing her knees against his side. In a tender, restrained voice she whispered, almost in his ear:

"Win, my beauty! Win me my soldier at West Point! Win me my love, my home, my father, and my freedom from the persecutions of this man! Fly on! Fly on, you 'Bird of the Desert'! Win, and Allah will bless you!"

She was stretched like an Indian along the back of her running horse.

Then—there they were at the end of the course, Morgan a full length ahead of Silvertail!

In an instant she was off and had buried her face in Morgan's mane; she was sobbing and laughing all at once, with her arms close about the horse's neck, as if she would never let him go!

Silvertail came up, a small spot of blood showing on his side where the cruel spur had wounded him.

Master Knickerbocker drew from his pocket a packet of papers, taking his defeat outwardly in better part than might have been expected.

"You have won, ma'am," he said in a low, hoarse voice, for he had much to do to control himself. "You have won, and that right fairly. I could have wished it otherwise, nor do I *yet* see how 'twas done! Your horse was better than mine, I suppose; and now I shall bid you good-bye, forever."

Mistress Lloyd took the packet in her trembling fingers; with her face still screened behind the Morgan, she said gently,

"Nay, but I must thank you for these——"

But she was interrupted, brusquely:

"There is naught to thank me for," he said, with truth. "Thank that Canadian scrub of yours. Since the race is over methinks I have tried conclusions with him before, many years back when we were both younger; I shall look to it that I am not deceived into competing with him again! That horse ought to be on The Plains of Abraham; he is wasted here!"

Mistress Lloyd extended her hand across the Morgan's neck, and Master Knickerbocker raised it to his lips with his usual grace; then he swung himself into his saddle and galloped out of sight.

FOOTNOTES:

[10] *Morgan Horses*, Linsley, page 134.

CHAPTER XVI.

IN WHICH MORGAN IS KNOWN
AS THE GOSS HORSE.

Soon after his race with Silvertail, Morgan's reputation, having spread so far, he was bought by Colonel John Goss, who, not caring to have the trouble of a horse himself, rode him over to St. Johnsbury, and loaned him to David Goss.

When they arrived it was the eve of Training Day, the second of June, and many farmers were gathered and making merry at the tavern. Having all heard of the Morgan, a great sensation was created as Colonel Goss rode him up to the porch of the Inn to show him off after Abel Shorey had trimmed and rubbed him down.

He had cantered gaily up—mane and tail waving, wide nostrils tremulous at new scents, alert ears pricking for new sounds.

Later he was ridden to his stable in David Goss's barn. The Goss place was a fine one, with large farmhouse, barn and outbuildings, the whole being surrounded by tall and stately trees.

It was a beautiful home for a horse to claim, and it was to be Morgan's for a long time. Here his name was changed again, and he became known as the Goss Horse, and was valued at one hundred dollars.

Under David's saddle he travelled more than ever to near-by towns and farms; he went to East Bethel, Williamstown, Greensboro and Claremont. In all of these places he was made welcome and, for a hundred years and more, men have been telling of these visits.

Sometimes David rode him to "raising parties," where he stood one side and watched strong young men lift the ponderous bents for the barn or house about to be built. They used pike-poles, and shouted loudly, lifting the bents one by one till the tenons sank into place in the sill-mortises; then, some dare-devil afraid-of-nothing, went up the new-hoisted bents like a squirrel and drove the pins into place.

While men worked this way, or at the plow, women sat at home and dipped candles or spun and wove flax and wool, and made them into clothes.

Those were grand days in Vermont—when neighbors were neighbors, and the world was full of hope and kindliness.

At this time Samuel Goss owned a newspaper called *The Montpelier Watchman,* and in its columns could be found notices of the endurance, beauty and gentleness of the Goss—but far from turning his level head, it only made him strive harder to deserve the praise. Modestly and cheerfully he went his way as farm-horse, saddle-horse, carriage-horse: always endearing himself to every one associated with him. It was his perfect training and his willingness to obey that was ever the secret of success of Justin Morgan.[11]

By this time Montpelier was growing so prosperous, being made the capital in 1808, that people began to think more of pleasure parties, and bees of all sorts were held. History gives the credit to Mistress Debbie Daphne Davis for inventing pumpkin pies, without a goodly supply of which no company was considered complete. Even Goss had his share of these, for every one paid him attentions when he waited outside a house for his rider. He found the pies very palatable, for at the kitchen windows of his women friends he had learned to appreciate many concoctions not usually known to horses.

Sometimes a lady rode him to meeting in St. Johnsbury.[12] The meeting house was little larger than his stall, and from where he waited he could hear the preacher shouting forth healthy doctrine in liberal measure with a strong flavor of brimstone. After this the congregation would rise, noisily, as with relief, and sing a hymn at the tops of their voices. Sometimes they sang "Mear," which ever reminded Morgan of the Randolph singing-teacher who had been his good friend, and whose name he once bore.

Vermonters were real Christians in those days and regulations regarding the keeping of the Holy Sabbath were enforced by tithing-men who walked among the people during Meeting to see that they behaved themselves in a seemly manner. If any one was caught asleep or inattentive, and a Christian whack over the head with a hymn-book did not waken him to a fitting sense of his responsibilities, a committee of Selectmen "waited" upon him the next day with results entirely satisfactory.

Such visits, however, were uncommon. The pioneers of Vermont were a law-abiding people, honest, thrifty, religious and possessing all the virtues that go to make up a strong, fine race.

That same year, 1808, Goss found himself in Burlington for a time, and had an adventure known in the history of Vermont, although his name has never before been recorded in connection with it.

One evening he went, under the saddle of a revenue officer, bent on a secret mission, to the mouth of the Winooski.

Chill and darkness settled on the forest, stars came out and they tarried at the farm of Ira Allen, at Rocky Point, until the great yellow moon swam into sight and other officers joined them.

Leaves rustled softly as they started out through the woods, an owl hooted solemnly, and from somewhere far off a whippoorwill called.

A short ride brought them to rugged rocks and rude cliffs over-hanging the river, in the then almost untouched forest, where Goss was left behind a sheltering boulder.

In a few moments he distinctly saw a boat floating on the quiet bosom of the water. The far-flung sound of men's voices came to him borne on the slight wind that sighed in the treetops. It was an in-expressibly lonely spot, and Goss shuddered once with a feeling of impending tragedy.

Having heard much talk of the Smuggler—"Black Snake"—for which the Government had been watching so long—with rum, brandy, and wines on board—it was not hard for him to guess why the officers were here.

As the vessel hove to, shadowy figures dropped from her side and began unloading kegs and indistinguishable objects. For a time deathly stillness reigned. Ever responsive to influences, Goss breathed softly, and did not sneeze. The officers stepped as lightly as cats, bracing themselves.

Suddenly there was the crackle of a musket from the bank, fol-lowed by others, then the boat answered, shot for shot. The woods blazed—the echoes woke. Bullets whistled through the trees above the horse, but he neither flinched nor whinneyed as the scattered leaves fell about him. After a while, quivering with subdued excite-ment, he strained his neck forward with dilating nostrils—he hoped it was a battle!

And it was—in a small way.

A man, poised on the deck of the "Black Snake," swayed and pitched head-first into the river and sank beneath the dark water. There were oaths and cries, then the "Black Snake" gathered sail and sped before the rising wind down the river and out of sight, followed by a volley of musketry.

This was but one of the many episodes of that border State, Ver-mont, which gave her an atmosphere of adventure and filled her young men with courage and her women with that quality of cool-ness which faces life and its cares unflinchingly.

A little later Goss saw several men advancing, tired, silent and grim. They were mountain men and stern, they had not much to say, but they bore between them the lifeless body of the officer who had so lately been the horse's pleasant rider.

Goss shivered as they placed their burden across his back.

As they set out wearily toward Burlington between crag and tree the dawn showed, coming over the mountain, spreading long shafts of crimson on the placid lake. Tahawas, towering above the former domains of the Iroquois Indians, reared his lofty head dimly in the distance through the dispersing mists.

Slowly they went through the forest over thick pine needles which deadened their steps, through vague shadowy dells where ferns grew rank and cool streams trickled; on through the pathless woods until finally they reached a farm-clearing, in the centre of which, set in a frame of apples trees, stood a long, low house. Reverently the men lifted the burden from the horse's back, and, with lowered heads and measured tread, they bore it into the house.

Goss waited patiently. He heard a robin singing in an apple tree among the rustling leaves. He watched a hairy woodpecker run up the side of a tree, using his bill as a pick-axe and scaling off bits of bark sideways as he ran, disturbing a squirrel who sprang nimbly from limb to limb. A meadow-lark dipped across the sky over level fields of delicious beans, maize and squashes; a partridge called from the distance and fleecy clouds floated across the now full-risen sun casting long shadows on the lake, like the spirit of Hiawatha's white canoe—to the southward grim Regiohne, gloomy sentinel of rock, kept guard. Around all the fine frame of mountains ranged.

In the golden morning sunshine Nature glowed with happiness. Then all at once a low sound came to Goss's pricking ears, the sound of a woman weeping, and a shadow fell across the doorway, as of an angel's wing.

* * * *

The Goss horse played his part, too, in many fine affairs. The following year at the inauguration of the Preacher-Governor, Jonas Galusha, he had the honor of carrying the newly-elected Chief Magistrate in the grand parade. Crowds shouted and cheered as they passed, drums were beaten and guns fired. Goss was almost as much noticed as the Governor himself!

The Executive spoke in the town hall, outside which the horse waited. Goss could hear the applause now and then, and when the speech was finished a wag cried out:

"Now let's sing 'Mear'!"

Every one knew that "Mear" was the Governor's favorite hymn, but instead of singing, as Goss hoped they would, an outburst of laughter greeted the suggestion, and the crowd poured noisily out into the street once more.

Goss had a good time that day prancing to the music and showing off. His enjoyment of such gay doings always made him popular with the men, yet so gentle was he that women constantly borrowed him to ride to meetings, quiltings, bees, or funerals.

At Burlington in this same year, 1809, the launching of the steamboat "Vermont" (of which they had talked so long) took place. The "Vermont" had been built *second* to the "Clermont" (launched on the Hudson, about two years before), but an unavoidable delay made her the *fifth* steamboat to be launched.

At great expense this passenger steamer had been built and was to run from White Hall to St. Johns in twenty-four hours! It was almost too much to ask the people to believe, said the newspapers! One and all they predicted failure. Steamboats in those days occupied much the same place in the estimation of the people as airships did a hundred years later. Many called it a foolish waste of money, and dangerous withal, but John Winans, who made the boat, was confident it would mark an epoch in history.

Larger and finer than the "Clermont," the success of the "Vermont" on Lake Champlain does not concern our hero.

The streets were crowded with passengers from the mail coaches; the Foote House was taxed to capacity; four-, six- and eight-horse teams, with now and then a Canadian spike-team, blocked the thoroughfares.

Into this atmosphere of excitement and interest David and Goss cantered early that morning, and put up at the house of Mr. Loomis. This historic house had sheltered His Royal Highness, Edward, Duke of Kent, who, in the year 1793, was travelling with his suite in sleighs from Boston to Canada. It was built of logs hewn out with a broad-axe and made a most warm and fitting place for so great a personage to tarry in, not less comfortable did our two more humble friends find it sixteen years later.

Nothing eventful occurred after the launching of the boat except that Goss met a horse from Maryland, who gave him news of Mistress Lloyd, now married to an army officer, known as the dashing Lieutenant Tom Dulaney.

The Southern horse told him also of the lately opened Baltimore course and of the great race there between Mr. Ogle's Oscar and First Consul, and how Oscar ran the second heat in the extraordinary time of 7:40, a speed that had never been exceeded for the same distance, and which seemed almost a miracle!

FOOTNOTES:

[11] "In the relations, duties, and pleasures of the road—and family-horse the Morgan has never had an equal in this country, no matter what his blood."—*John Wallace, Wallace's Monthly.*

[12] "I have always admired the Morgans. I believe that no family of horses has ever been produced which possesses in a high degree so many valuable qualities which go to make up an ideal gentleman's roadster, a family, or all-purpose horse, as the family founded by Justin Morgan."—*S. W. Parlin, Editor, American Horse Breeder.*

CHAPTER XVII.

IN THE FLOOD OF 1811.

In 1811 Samuel Stone bought the little horse and changed his name back to Morgan. Once more he went to live in Randolph, which had been the scene of his early triumphs.

There had been many changes in the town, and nearly all his old friends had moved away or outgrown their interest in tests of strength and speed. Only one of them was left, James Kelsey, and he, being fond of horses, often rode Morgan from place to place for Stone.

Kelsey was called the village "cut-up," though he was no longer a boy, but he had a kind heart and was the friend of every one. Sometimes he rode the Morgan alongside the stage-coaches and thrilled the passengers with stories of pioneer times; of bears, and Indians.

One day, as they were nearing Tunbridge, Kelsey told them of the burning of that place by three hundred Indians, who swept down from the north under the command of a British soldier, Lieutenant Horton.

This reference to the British reminded Morgan of his old enemy, the Tory boy, whose dog had killed Black Baby. The boy must now have reached man's estate, and Morgan wondered if he would recognize him if he saw him, and if Allah was planning an opportunity for him to give his promised kick. In all these years he had never forgotten his vow.

Kelsey was a very skillful rider, and could do wonderful things from a horse's back, which Morgan enjoyed, for it showed off his smooth and easy gaits. Sometimes, after slipping off his heavy boots and tying them to his stirrup, he would spring to his feet on the horse's back, and stand balancing himself while Morgan glided evenly along under him; or, riding hard, he would stoop and pick up a stone or stick; or, if there chanced to be a pretty flower beside the road, he would set the horse running and lean swiftly down, pluck the flower, and wait for the coach to catch up, that he might hand it to some lady passenger, with a bow and sweep of his hat.

One of his anecdotes, which always brought a laugh from the passengers—especially if they were from New York—was how the tract of land, now known as Vermont, was granted to Dominie Dillius, of Albany, in 1696, for the "annuall rente of one racoon skinne."

"The New York legislature," Kelsey always finished, "later called this 'rente' *excessive!*"

During that spring there came a scourge of locusts. They ate up the trees and all green things. Wise old women declared them a sign of coming disaster—disaster enough they were of themselves! With their strident cries they drowned the prayers of the Righteous who sat in meeting praying to be delivered from them and their consequences.

One day at noon a darkness fell over everything; cocks crew; pigs squealed; cows came home, lowing; dogs howled, dismally; and cats mewed, distressingly.

Morgan, sensitive to all influences, shivered and moaned, softly.

One of the most fearsome calamities in the history of Vermont was, indeed, about to descend.

Masses of clouds rose and blotted out the sun; the storm came closer; thunder crashed; the wind howled; rain began to fall.

Day after day lightning flashed, thunder jarred the earth, and the rain fell unceasingly. There seemed no end to it!

Creek and river beds lost all identity; mountains were obscured in the downpour. In lowlands, beaver meadows and swampy places the water rose, and kept rising. Mountain streams became torrents, creeks became rivers.

It was a deluge!

Birds, drenched through their feathers, starved and fell to the earth, chilled to death; insects were washed out of the air; late-hatched broods of wild ducks were drowned and the eggs of wild-fowl floated on the surface of the waters.

Weasels, stoats and such creatures as could swim reached higher ground and for a short time saved their lives. Cattle, which had sought slightly dryer quarters on hillocks, were drowned as they called aloud, piteously, for help. Field-mice, rabbits and moles were suffocated in the rain-sodden earth. Foxes climbed into bushes to await the going down of the waters and were drowned, or starved to death, waiting.

This was the year men praised the Lord for directing them to build their towns on hills, for they were thus above the valley floods that poured towards the Connecticut or the lake. But all about their homes the pine-needles and underbrush held the water like a sponge.

On one of the very worst nights of the "flood" Samuel Stone set out to help a neighbor rescue his cattle.

Stone apologized to Morgan for taking him out on such a night, with thunder and lightning so terrible.

"'Tis hard to go out in such weather, Pony, but we must help our neighbors in their troubles, else when we are in straits they will not come to us!"

The dense blackness and silence that followed the rapid flashes of orange lightning and roaring thunder—and his natural terror of storms—confused Morgan's sight and hearing.

Fortunately, however, he had never had rheumatism, nor stiffness of any kind, and his reluctance to leave his leaky stable was counteracted by his desire to do his duty bravely.

Trusting blindly in his master's judgment, he cantered off.

The wind blew and whistled like evil spirits, the swaying trees bent almost to the ground, but at last they reached the neighbor's house and succeeded in saving his terrified cattle, though with great difficulty. Afterwards the neighbor besought them to pass the night, but Stone refused, saying that, "by morning the bridges would all be gone and they must be getting home-along before that happened!"

Hurriedly partaking of a hot supper in the leaking kitchen, near a sputtering fire, and after giving Morgan a good, warm mash, Stone mounted and rode away into the storm and night.

Darkness fell about them like a blanket; there was nothing for the rider to do but leave it to his horse's instinct and sense of direction to take him home.

Not once did Justin Morgan hesitate.

Very soon, by the roar of water the horse knew they were near Beaver Creek, a torrent, rising high in the mountains, and gathering strength as it raced and tore to the valley through narrow gorges, was now a raging cataract. In crossing this stream earlier, Morgan had perceived that the bridge could not last much longer; he had felt the timbers tremble under his tread.

Now, several hours later, he could hear the current, more angry than before, whirling its mass of foam and *débris* against the banks. As they reached the place where the bridge ought to have been not a ray of starlight showed Stone it was no longer there. But involuntarily, he refrained from guiding or suggesting to the horse any course of action. The reins lay loose even when Morgan paused at the brink of the torrent.

Leaning forward, Stone patted the horse's neck gently, and said in a soothing voice:

"Steady, Boy, steady!"

Morgan responded.

He could see with his keen eyes, the white, turbid water, below the very place where the bridge had been—one stringer alone of the structure remained, and this was scarce above the violent current! The rushing, churning water swirled against the banks impetuously.

Cautiously, the horse tried the wide beam with one foot. Feeling it secure, he tried another; in the inky darkness, he pushed his feet along gently, lest he step on an upstanding nail.

Steadily, firmly, without wavering, without—above all—interference from his rider, he went on over the spinning foam on his narrow foot-bridge.

At last he put his foot on solid ground and, with a slight, throaty sound of relief, he cantered briskly off toward home.

As they neared the house he whinneyed, as was his custom, and Mistress Stone threw open the door and stood silhouetted against the radiance from within. The glow of firelight penetrated the darkness, and from a guttering candle, held high above her head, a tiny beam of welcome went out to her good man.

"Oh, Samuel," she cried, right joyfully, "'tis a great comfort to hear your voice again! By what road came you back?"

"By Beaver Creek Road, wife," he made answer.

"But, look you, the bridge is gone—how crossed you the creek?"

"By the bridge, all the same—'twas not gone five minutes ago."

"But, indeed, 'tis washed away a long time since," his wife cried, in amazement, "for James Kelsey came by these two hours agone and told me he had but just crossed in time. Scarce had he landed on this side when there was a great crashing and grinding of timbers and the whole thing was swept away before his very eyes! He saw by a flash of lightning—all went but one stringer which was wedged against the rocks at either end!"

And, marvelling together, they fed the "pony" as befitted a hero, though Morgan looked upon it as but an incident in the day's work and went about his delicious supper with placid forgetfulness of all else.

CHAPTER XVIII.

UNDER CAPTAIN DULANEY.

Then one day the sun rose clear and bright, the waters sank and the mountains showed clean-cut against the fleckless sky—but no bees buzzed, no sweet odors filled the air, no wild flowers carpeted the woods, no butterflies fluttered, no birds sang.

Vermont tasted that year the bitter cup of desolation.

A dire scourge of spotted fever, or "plague," the doctors called it, broke out, severest in Montpelier. Consternation was great among the Sabbath-abiding folk who claimed solemnly that the affliction was due to the worldly ways and "flunk and flummux" of the "foreigners" who came from other states to pass the summer in the Green Mountains. Even the women of Vermont, themselves, had taken to wearing laces, ribbands, frills and furbelows—most unbecoming in God-fearing females!

Stagnant water stood in pools, here and there, houses were damp, there were no crops, and all food was mouldy and unwholesome, for lack of sunshine.

In Montpelier men went from house to house, carrying long bathing vessels, and such of the women as had not yet been attacked with the "plague" bathed the stricken ones in an infusion of hemlock boughs. Doctors bled them and dosed them with teas more or less harmful made of ginseng, pleurisy-root and marshmallow. Fresh air, sunshine and pure water with proper nourishment would have been better, but in those days bleeding and herb-teas were the two panaceas for all ills.

In Williston, Dame Susannah Wells, who had reached the ripe age of one hundred and four years and seen her descendants die year after year of old age—without warning fell ill with the plague and died. Had it not been for this her acquaintances had long since come to the conclusion she would have lived forever. Children and babies were mowed down with equal impartiality by the Reaper; men and women succumbed; but Morgan's hardihood saved him from any ill effects of the long, wet season.

Events in his life, following 1811, were not of great importance and may be passed over until Stone put him up for sale in Burlington, at the stable of the Rev. Daniel Clark Sanders, President of the fine College on the hill. There he stayed for a long time, as he was growing old, they said, and no one wanted to buy him. President Sanders was quite willing, for he had the use and care of him all that while. Now and then Stone came to the stable with a prospective buyer, but a trade was never consummated.

As a convenient dooryard Ira Allen had given a space of fifty acres around the College, called The Green. It was still full of stumps and piles of brush, but made a delightful place for the cows and horses of the town to graze, and here Morgan had many agreeable experiences.

The merry students, passing by, gave him friendly greeting always and a dainty of some kind from their lunches; he learned to know the whistle of many and whinneyed to them as they ran toward him.

Often, as he stood nibbling grass he saw a strange looking youth limp across the Green with never a nod or greeting for him or any one else. Absorbed, stern of expression, and morose, this lad was destined to rise to prominence, the like of which could not be foreseen in one without influence, the son of a poor, hard working widow. This lame boy was none other than young Thaddeus Stevens, who, by industry and perseverance, gained his book-learning in Burlington and later graduated at Dartmouth College.

Burlington was now a very different place from the logging camp Morgan first remembered. The old wharf, made of a few logs fastened together, at the foot of King's Street, had given way to a fine new one; houses had taken the place of camps and were scattered as far as the Winooski.

The College on the Hill, commanding the lake, gave distinction to the town, seeming to crown it with a cap of learning; Ira Allen's iron foundries, mills and forges gave work to many, and linen, woolen and cotton mills had been built; an immense quantity of liquor was distilled. It was a busy and prosperous town, having grown greatly in importance since Ira Allen launched his first schooner, "Liberty," a long while before.

One day Stone brought to the stable an army officer. The military hat was set well upon the handsome head of the stranger, a cloak was flung with careless grace about his shoulder; spurs shone on his heels and a sword clanked, musically, at his side.

Intuitively, Morgan liked this man. It was easy to see he was a fine, brave American soldier, with a cool and level head. His uniform was grand and inspiring to the horse, who still looked upon soldiers and the idea of war with quivering anticipation.

"So this is the horse, eh?" the officer asked Stone, and Morgan knew by his soft tone and speech that he came from the same state as Mistress Lloyd—there was no mistaking a Marylander! As the stranger caught the halter his touch was so firm and friendly the horse knew instantly that here was his *master*. He arched his crest, pawed the ground prettily, and thrust his large, sensitive nostrils forward.

Stone led him out into the bright sunshine; the officer examined him thoroughly—an operation Morgan had long since grown accustomed to, as he had changed owners so often.

A flame of friendship sprang up between the two.

"I can scarce credit his age to be twenty-two!" said the stranger. "He has such suppleness of joint, he moves with the action of a five-year-old!"

Stone was pleased and proud of his horse; he said:

"Those are his characteristics, Captain Dulaney!"

Dulaney? Morgan's memory awoke, vaguely.

"And from what stock, did you say?" the officer enquired.

Stone let him know all that was said concerning Morgan's parentage. Then he continued:

"He has worked hard at the plow, most of his life, and he is not known in horse-books, but we Vermonters don't take much interest in pedigrees. We say, 'pretty is as pretty does' and present merit is what we go by, Captain—not what his *ancestors* did!"

The Maryland gentleman laughed, seeing the point.

"Blood speaks for itself, right here," Captain Dulaney said. "I will wager my new sword that this horse has thoroughbred blood! So you see your argument about pedigree does not hold!"

Morgan waved his tail slightly, in acknowledgment.

"I like the animal," added the Captain, in his quiet, pleasant way. "I would mount him, sir."

In ten minutes Morgan was accoutred in the military trappings and saddle of an officer of the United States Army. It was with a thrill that he felt the Captain throw his fine-dressed leg across his back and slip his cavalry-booted feet into the stirrups—all the while holding the reins in his masterful hand. A mutual confidence was awakened between the two that was to last always.

Morgan, feeling as young as he did ten years before, cantered smoothly off, side-stepping just enough to give his rider something to do.

Down the hill they went, the horse as sure-footed as a goat, feeling that he had never carried so dashing and gallant a rider nor so congenial a spirit, and right glad was he to respond to every gentle pressure of the bit or motion of the rein.

At the turn of the trail they came to a stone fence. At his rider's suggestion Morgan paused slightly, pulled himself together, rose in the air and cleared it. Over a rushing little stream he went in the same confident, bird-like way, galloping easily off as he touched the ground on the other side.

The blue sky was reflected in the lake, and the mountains in New York pierced it, in reality, or reflection, with peaks of green and brown. The air was still and pure and the cool scent of the pines was strong in their nostrils. The haze of the morning had given place to a crystal clearness and Juniper Island was like a spot of precious jade set in a field of turquoise.

They were on the way to the Falls at a smart gallop now, and what his rider intimated to the horse along the bridle-rein gave him courage and love combined with perfect understanding. At a convenient spot they stopped, and Captain Dulaney spoke aloud.

"Ah, my fine fellow!" Morgan flicked his tail in reply, and tossed his mane slightly—with an up and down motion once or twice of his crest as was his habit when spoken to, directly—"Ah, my fine fellow, this air makes one breathe deeply. There's no climate like it. No wonder these Vermonters are giants morally and physically. No wonder the Green Mountain Boys could take Ticonderoga! A handful of men bred in this air are worth all the city-bred officers in the British Army. And forsooth, they proved it! Ha! Ha! If it comes to an attack by water from Canada on the lake, here, we have a superabundance of trained officers and men."

He dismounted and spread a map on the ground, weighting the corners with pink and red fragments of stones picked up at random. Had he known it, these were pieces of marble, later to make that locality famous, when the quarries were discovered.

In silence he studied the map, the bridle rein hanging across his arm. Then he folded it, sprang suddenly into the saddle and continued his thinking aloud as they started off:

"Now if we could be sure of the Vermonters in this war, but they seem to think fighting foolish—and in this they may be right, eh, Morgan? New England is in a ferment, but we've got to stick by the President and fight it out. Although they call it 'Mr. Madison's War,' that poor man is the most unwilling participant in it! The thing is to find which way the cat will jump here; that's my business. These secret emissaries from England and Canada may be right here now, rousing the Vermonters to join Canada. But may be the sight of a good old Continental uniform—God bless it!—may bring them our way!"

The lake glinted blue in the sunshine, the birds twittered in the forest, as they passed on slowly.

Suddenly Captain Dulaney addressed the horse gaily:

"Look at that view, Morgan. Shall we let a king wrest it from us? No, I swear it! This air is like wine. Who would live in towns, say I, with houses crowding, one upon the other, peeping over each other's heads to see the narrow streets that lie between? Not I, for one. Give me trees and sky, rivers and fields, and the green country down in Maryland, 'Where the Great Lloyd sets his Hall.'"

Morgan started. He turned his straight, intelligent face full round and looked at his rider. A smile, quick and magnetic, met his dark, prominent eye. Then a light flooded his horse mind. No wonder he loved this officer! Had he not won him for Mistress Lloyd so long ago? He remembered all now. From the tip of his tail to his fine, sharp ears he quivered with happiness. Maybe after a life-time of waiting he would see her again!

Overhead the sky was cloudless, but suddenly across its face came sweeping into view, over-shadowing the woods for a moment, a dense flock of wild pigeons. The Captain leaned forward and patted Morgan's neck.

"Just pigeons, old man! Is that why you shivered? Or is there something you want to say?"

But Morgan could not answer in words, he could only hope and serve. He did wish, however, that Captain Dulaney would not call him "old"! He had years of usefulness before him yet!

"I wish my sweet wife were here now to enjoy this view with us!"

Morgan replied with a toss of his head.

"But she is coming!"

Morgan whinneyed, softly, and trembled all over.

"God bless her!" went on the Captain, his blue eyes deepening to a light, wholly tender, "She would scarce consent to my coming up here without her. She argued with me, the witch, that Mistress Washington had passed the winter at Valley Forge, and she did not love her General any more than my wife loved her Captain! It was a clinching argument, Morgan, my friend, and I had to promise that she should come when all was ready—and there she is waiting in Boston until I send for her."

Morgan tossed his head, and his tail waved slightly.

"She shall ride you, little horse, for, by my sword, there never was a more delightful, under the saddle. My mind is made up, I shall buy you, old as you are!"

There it was again—"As old as you are." Age! what has age to do with it if the heart and spirit are young?

"As for these Vermonters," the Captain continued, thinking aloud, and riding on, "they are brave, fine men and they will stand by Ethan Allen's ideals; if war comes they will be with us. I've felt the pulse of Vermont from North to South, and I believe in them in spite of their reserve and non-committal attitude."

They galloped on over rocky, new-cleared spaces, across streams and fences, and pushed their way slowly through underbrush. When they stopped, Dulaney pulled Morgan's lean head round and caught his bright, pleasant eye. The Captain winked at him with a chuckle.

"We'll win this war yet——"

So there was to be a war! Morgan's pupils dilated, his nostrils spread.

"Yes, we'll win this war, as we did the other," and the officer nodded his head with conviction. "I was but a lad of ten, Morgan, when we heard of Cornwallis' surrender, in 1781. 'Twas a crisp autumn day and I well recall the shouting and hurrahing, the patriotic acclamations and glowing ardor of the Americans.

"To-day we have no Washington, no Hamilton, no La Fayette. We can but wait and see. But to me it seems a foregone conclusion. We have the larger ships, the heavier ordnance, and we are superior in seamanship and gunnery. Our vessels are few, but equipped thoroughly. Right will prevail—and we are right, aren't we, Morgan?"

Having finished his somewhat whimsical remarks, he wheeled his horse once more, and galloped toward Rocky Point where he stopped long—taking further observations of lake and country, turning in his saddle and gazing with thoughtful brow in every direction, scanning the horizon line, the lake, the streams, the roads.

Before the day was done they had skirted the rugged coast and crossed the sand-bar to La Grande Isle. So great was the number of salmon in those days that, as Morgan waded knee-deep in the water among them, they splashed away from his feet, as if in play.

Squirrels ran over the ground on the island and chattered down at them from the boughs. Clear and deep the blue lake lay, the woods coming to the very edge where poplars trembled in the clear light and tall, straight white-pines towered like sentinels.

From Island Point they could see Plattsburg Harbor, and here Captain Dulaney again sat for a long time buried in thought, looking across the wild, dark forest and lake.

At dusk they bent their faces homeward, both horse and rider absorbed in his own meditations until they reached College Hill.

Early next morning Samuel Stone came to bid the Morgan goodbye, telling him he had been bought by Captain Dulaney, and that he "was a very lucky horse!" Morgan knew this far better than Stone—wasn't Mistress Dulaney coming, and would he not have the happiness of cantering under her saddle once more?

But she did not come at once. During the fall and winter of 1812 and 1813, the United States troops arrived and were settled in the College buildings, now called United States Barracks for the winter.

Captain Dulaney rode Morgan daily and taught him to be a true cavalry horse and to obey bugle calls. So obedient did he become and so conscientious was he, that, one day when he was attached to a "shay" at the foot of the hill, he heard the bugle sound "Charge." He obeyed instantly on the impulse, snapping his hitch rein sharply. Up the hill he "charged" at full speed, the shay rattling on behind! 'Twas not his fault that it was not shaken into bits! From a colt it had been his instinct to obey without question, and certainly, at last, in the service of his country he did not hesitate!

Soldiers, off duty, lounging idly in the shade, roused themselves with a great roar of laughter as the old horse charged toward them. An orderly sprang forward and caught the bit. Not a strap, not a tug was broken! Every one cheered heartily, for "Old Justin Morgan" had come to be a character at the post and was loved by all, men as well as officers.

Time passed and still Mistress Dulaney did not come, though every day Morgan looked for the one great, human love of his life. He wondered if she remembered him—if she recalled the part he had played in freeing her from the Coxcomb, and winning her the man she loved.

In the spring of 1813, when the ice broke up, a fleet was fitted out. Oak timbers, cut on the Winooski, were sawed at the mills, nails and bolts were fashioned out of hot iron at the forges where even the bellows breathed patriotism. Masts and spars were tapered and sails made. Liberty poles were set up on eminences—the higher the pole the stronger the patriotism. Everything indicated war.

Commodore Macdonough took command of the lake and naval stores and ammunition arrived from the South. All seemed waiting for the call to arms when an epidemic of lung-fever broke out among the troops stationed at the barracks.

Captain Dulaney was stricken, and lay ill unto death at his quarters. Morgan missed him and pined for his company.

A letter was dispatched to Mistress Dulaney, but the distance to Boston was so great that a man might die before the stage went and returned to Burlington. At last when the coach rattled up, with a great noise and hurly-burly, to the officer's quarters and stopped, all knew that Mistress Dulaney was inside, and it chanced that Morgan stood hitched near-by. The steps were quickly let down and right quickly did she descend.

Morgan recognized her at once; he whinneyed a note of welcome, but she neither saw nor heard him; she was in such stress of anxiety.

She was all his memory held her: not so young, but more sweet, more beautiful and a light as of a halo surrounded her face as they told her the Captain was better. Morgan saw all before she put her little foot to the ground.

But as she hurried into the house the horse felt old, a sudden darkness fell upon the world, as if a cloud had obscured the sun.

She had not even *seen* him!

He hung his head and tears filled his dear, longing eyes. After all these years of waiting and loving—and she had not even seen him!

CHAPTER XIX.

MORGAN MEETS HIS LADY AGAIN.

But Captain Dulaney did not die of the "lung fever," as so many did. He was made for a nobler end and had work yet to do.

The mutterings of war came ever nearer and nearer to Lake Champlain and crowded out all other thoughts and interests.

Morgan waited two weeks for a sight of his Lady. Nobody came to tell him the news, so he could only hope the Captain would recover and need to go for an airing after a while.

One day the orderly, a mannerly youth whom horses liked, groomed him so carefully that the old horse guessed the airing he had looked forward to was about to take place.

He was scarcely able to control his impatience as he stood at the step waiting. He was sure she would see him this time, and he trembled with longing, and the hope that she had not forgotten him.

* * * *

She came down the steps slowly, the Captain, a little weak still, leaning on her arm, yet not entirely for support—a little for the joy of laying his thin, white hand on her strong, steady one.

At last, as her husband spoke, she raised her eyes.

"This is the horse I've written you so much about, my Hollyhock!"

She knew him at once!

"Why, my dear! 'Tis the very horse that won you for me!" she cried, joyfully; she might forget a person—his lady—but never a horse. "Why did you not tell me so before? I have asked so often about him, and 'twould have brought me to Vermont before this!"

The Captain smiled.

"I shall be jealous of my charger," he said, tenderly.

Morgan rubbed his muzzle on Mistress Dulaney's sleeve and in the laces at her neck, thinking her soft Southern voice the sweetest he had ever heard, even more sweet than when she was a maid.

"Ah, dear husband, but for this horse I should be the most unhappy of women instead of the happiest! 'Twas he who won that race so many years ago and gave you to me. I have ever wanted to call him my own!"

"Then you may call him so now, sweet Wife. From to-day Morgan is yours."

At last, at last! Oh, the years of waiting and longing. Oh, the weary hopelessness of some of them at the plow-among men who could not understand and did not try. At last! He arched his crest and pawed the earth with joy.

"I shall lend him to you sometimes." She looked at her lord, archly lifting her sweet face to his as they stood very close together. At a soft, sweet sound Morgan showed more spirit.

"'He paweth in the valley and rejoiceth in his strength; he goeth forth to meet the armed men,'" Mistress Dulaney quoted, mockingly, her hand resting on the horse's face, her cheek against his.

Presently the Captain mounted, lighter by several pounds than was his wont, and Morgan glided off.

"Take good care of him, Little Horse," were her parting words.

* * * *

Early that summer, when the feeling of victory was running high, the American Sloop of War, "Growler," was captured by the British gun-boats on the Upper Lake. The Americans equipped a small fleet and drove the enemy back into Canada.

The State Militia, stationed at Plattsburg, was ordered home in November, by Governor Chittenden, but most of the officers remained. The privates—from the first, unwilling to enlist—were glad enough to return to their families who needed them sorely. They would much rather chop and dig at home, they said, having found nothing to do in Plattsburg but repair the barracks.

Every day Captain or Mistress Dulaney rode Morgan out for exercise, and he enjoyed the easy, pleasant life with its military atmosphere. His lady visited him every morning early and gave him many delicious morsels of food, and the old horse seemed to grow younger day by day. She talked to him of all sorts of interesting things in tones, so wonderfully sweet, the birds in the Green Mountains would have died of envy, could they have heard them.

Sometimes errands with Captain Dulaney were of great secrecy and importance. One night quite late they went away toward the North and passed the night at a barn, watching a suspicious locality. As they were about to start homeward, the Captain searched carefully and found a furled flag, lying on a beam. He took it down and unrolled it, looking for secret signs, but the flag was right enough. It was made of the finest linen, home-spun, and was fifteen feet long by four wide. In its centre was an eagle perched on a rock, bearing in its talons a shield with thirteen stripes and some arrows. In his beak was a pine sprig, and over the eagle was painted "Independence Forever." The word "Swanton" was painted on it in another hand.

As Captain Dulaney noticed the last word he said to himself, with relief:

"'Tis well! We've nothing to fear. Lieutenant Van Sicklen was right. The people in this locality are patriots. He will return this way, perhaps, so I shall put the flag back with my private mark."[13]

He made a certain distinguishing mark and laid the flag back on the sill.

A strange event occurred on their way home through the darkness.

Suddenly there was a hissing, as of red hot iron thrust into water, a familiar sound to Morgan who had lived so long near a forge, and then there came a violent explosion. The earth fairly shook, and the horse felt his rider start in the saddle. He himself was so taken by surprise that he stopped so sharply his hoofs plowed great furrows in the ground.

Then Captain Dulaney spoke, and the sound of his steady voice quieted him.

"'Tis but a mass of iron fallen from space, old fellow—a meteor, they call it—a rare and interesting sight if one happens to be far enough away! Any nearer for us might have made Mistress Dulaney a widow without a riding horse!" He laughed reassuringly. "We will show the British a few stars like that at shorter range, pretty soon. What say you?"

Morgan waved his tail.

Next day folk went from everywhere to see the "fallen star," and wise old women—who infested every community at that time—said it was an ill-omen, and meant victory for the British!

In the spring of 1814, the American Squadron lay in Otter Creek, which, flowing gently toward the lake, afforded safe anchorage for the vessels. In May as they were about to quit port, the enemy approached off the mouth of the creek with a well-matured plan to "bottle them up" by sinking two sloops filled with stones in the channel. But the Americans fired and frightened them off before they had played their clever trick.

In the middle of August the "Eagle" was launched and the murmur arose, "the British are gathering on the frontier."

104

On September third began the real excitement. Before cock-crow the whole place was astir. Morgan, feeling the influence, was scarcely able to eat his breakfast. But when he finally finished, and was led out, the barracks were alive with soldiers and officers. Morgan champed his bit—ready to be gone on any errand that was needed. Seconds passed slowly, he was so eager to be off! In a few moments Lieutenant Van Sicklen sprang out of a near-by door, and gathering the reins in his hands swung himself into the saddle.

The old horse was off like a shot toward the goal, wherever it was, his rider close to his neck, talking to him as a lady-love might, whispering words of encouragement and affection.

They dashed down the hill at such speed that an old cow, lying comfortably in the road, chewing her morning cud, had the experience of acting as a hurdle. Seeing she could not possibly rise in time, the young officer gave Morgan the signal and over her they went! When she had recovered her stupid senses they were out of sight.

At last the hopes of the old horse were realized. He was serving his country and very soon understood the errand on which they were bent. He spurned the earth; stone fences stretched across his way; streams had to be forded; now and then a steep declivity appeared, but he was a "Bay," and he remembered what they say of a bay in the Desert; rough fields, retarding forests, and wide stretches of valley did not discourage him. Hurrying on he found naught but broad, fine happiness. He was serving his country!

White with foam he reached Hinesburg and Lieut. Van Sicklen shouted:

"The British are coming!"

Then over his shoulder:

"They have invaded Plattsburg and volunteers are wanted! On to Burlington!"

Every mouth took up the cry.

"On to Burlington, the British are coming!"

Morgan's nostrils showed red—but he was just beginning this wonderful experience, for which he had waited so long. On, on, to serve his country!

They left the people hurrying into their houses for their muskets. Men snatched them from the high mantel-shelves and started out leaving their plows stuck in the earth. The women did not weep—they, too, set out, some doggedly, some eager; they begged extra guns and went along leaving their kitchen doors open and their pots hanging from the cranes; they had not forgotten the Indians—and that other cry: "The British are coming!"

105

These were living memories to many. Even the children pleaded to go along, for was not the American spirit born in them?

And on Morgan and his rider went.

"The British are coming!"

The cry rose and fell and echoed through the mountains and valleys of Vermont.

At last they reached Montpelier where they were to rest the night at the Farmer's Inn, where Morgan used to live. But he was so tired he could not revive memories of his youth, and lay down on the clean straw to rest, almost at once.

He did not know how long he had been sleeping when his keen ears were penetrated by the whisper of men outside the stable door. He sprang to his four feet, suspiciously.

"'Tis the fleetest horse in the state," said one voice. "Have him out and you will signal General Prevost from the Upper Lake tomorrow night!"

"Prevost! a Red-Coat General!" thought Morgan. "They must be spies!"

The door was opened softly a moment later, and a man crept in.

On the instant a rush of air from without swept into Morgan's nostrils the unforgotten odor of the Tory Boy whose dog had killed Black Baby, the lamb. No longer a boy, he no doubt deserved the kick in accordance with his increased age and wickedness.

Here surely was the opportunity Allah had been preparing all these years.

Morgan had been standing with his face to the door, but, on recognizing the intruder, he wheeled suddenly, and with a cry, almost human, he delivered the kick of a lifetime!

Lieutenant Van Sicklen, sleeping near at hand and ever on the alert, had been roused by Morgan's first movement and rushed out with drawn sword. He reached the open door just in time to receive in his arms the limp form of the Tory spy.

The American officer was not too surprised to grasp him by the collar:

"How, now, sirrah! You would steal my horse, would you? We will soon quiet you and your kind!" Still holding him firmly—though the man was unconscious and unable to stand—he called, "What, ho! Within! I have no time to deal with spies or horse thieves! Come out and punish this fellow, if he is alive, according to your Vermont laws before you go to fight his peers!"

Nor did he and Morgan remain to see the fate of the Tory spy. They knew he would be dealt with according to his deserts.

FOOTNOTES:

[13] In December, 1907, a furled flag, covered with dust and dirt, and exactly answering the description of the flag examined by Captain Dulaney, was discovered on the sill of an old barn on what is now known as the Jed Mack Farm, at Swanton Junction, Vermont. The flag was old—even in 1814—for there were but thirteen stripes on it, and had been made before Vermont was admitted to the Union.

The finding of the flag nearly a century later proves that Lieut. Van Sicklen did not return that way and accounts for the discovery of the flag so long afterwards.

CHAPTER XX.

THE NAVAL BATTLE.

From Montpelier other messengers were sent in all directions to warn the farmers, and Lieut. Van Sicklen pushed on to Randolph, Morgan's old home. His former friends along the way would never have believed it, had they not known his age. Full twenty-five years old, he was yet eager, and, hard as the riding had been, not once had he faltered.

Whilst he waited in Randolph, Lieut. Van Sicklen, amidst roars of applause, roused the people to rally round the flag, and made such a patriotic speech from the porch of Dr. Timothy Baylies' Tavern, that the assembled crowd was carried away by his enthusiasm and shouted, wildly:

"Down with the British!"

It was a fire of patriotism burning high and clear, lighting the state from North to South.

Presently, on foot, on horseback, in wagons and in "shays," they swept out into the winding highways and headed toward Montpelier, where the Government arms were stored, with a great cracking of whips and cheering.

Eighty-five volunteers went from Randolph, with Captain Egerton Lebbins in command. In a fine fever of enthusiasm they were as splendid a set of men as Morgan had come across in his journey, showing much heroism and ardor, but their clothes were odd to see, goodness knows! One thing and another thrown on at random; but not once did it occur to any of them to doubt the propriety of the strange costumes.

Fortunate ones had entire buff and blue Continental uniforms, inherited from father or grandfather or once worn by themselves—which was a proud boast—some were stained darkly, telling the tale of another war. Others had brass buttons hastily sewn on their everyday coats. Still others had but one button—a sort of badge—but these were great treasures, for did they not bear the inscription, "Long live our President," and did they not have his initials—G. W.—on them?

Their arms, when they started out, were as varied as their coats.

Hunting knives, long muskets, spears made at the forge, of scraps of iron tied to oak staffs with raw hide, Indian arrow heads stuck into short hickory handles, and such like.

But after all, the wonder was that they could get together any sort of suggestive garb, or cared to—New England being in such a fever of dissatisfaction over the war.

Their mission completed, Lieut. Van Sicklen and Morgan returned to Burlington, and the day following this, Captain Dulaney rode his horse down to the wharf and, with many other officers, boarded the boat for Plattsburg.

The leaky old sloop, used to convey Captain Lebbins' "heroes" across, was washed up on Juniper Island in a storm of rain, and great was the anxiety concerning the brave fellows. A life boat was hurriedly manned and sent to their rescue—instead of finding the soldiers *perishing properly*, in true shipwreck fashion, the life-saving party found them celebrating their patriotism with Medford rum, high and dry on the island! "The wreck of Juniper Island" was the subject of many a song and story for long years in Randolph.

Commodore Macdonough's fleet was anchored off Plattsburg with fourteen vessels and eighty-six guns. On shore could be heard from the deck of his flagship, "Saratoga," the Commodore giving orders, in that cool, calm voice—so loved by Decatur and Bainbridge—the voice that indicated at once courage, humanity and confidence. Nor were these qualities at all disturbed by the rumor that a "host was advancing down the lake to crush the Yankees!"

The "host" was Captain George Downie, on his flagship, "Confiance," with a flotilla of sixteen vessels carrying ninety-two guns.

It was now the eve of a great naval engagement—the tenth of September, eighteen hundred and fourteen—the story of which has been told over and over for generations.

Near Captain Dulaney's headquarters, Morgan slept little that night; across the lake Burlington throbbed with flaring lights, and the town about him was wide awake. He dreamed waking dreams of his ancestor, the Turk, ridden by Captain Byerly, in King William's wars, one hundred and twenty-five years before—the Byerly Turk, he was called—who had seen the glories of Londonderry and Enniskillan.

Of another ancestor, too, he dreamed, the White Turk, ridden by Oliver Cromwell; and now he, Morgan, was taking part in a war under the saddle of his Lady's soldier—for this reason an even greater personage than Captain Byerly or Oliver Cromwell!

Long before dawn on the eleventh, his owner rode him out to

watch the maneuvers on the lake from an eminence, for it now seemed that Morgan was not to take an active part in this battle.

Commodore Macdonough had drawn his fleet up in two lines, forty yards apart, and as daylight came, and the morning advanced, the force weighed anchor and moved forward in a body. The wind was fair and at eight bells all was ready for the approaching ene-my—not more than a league away.

As the British ships came nearer the Americans swung their broadsides to bear—an intense stillness fell whose influence extend-ed to the watchers on land.

The "Saratoga" was silent—waiting—every man at his post, every nerve at the highest tension—some in fear, some in restraint, some in suspense—but every ear astrain against the rending of that awful silence.

And suddenly it was rent!

A cock, escaped from a coop, having mounted a gun-slide, on the "Saratoga," stretched his neck, flapped his wings, and crowed!

His defiance of the British was answered with a rousing cheer—the strain was broken—the depressed revived!

It was an omen presaging Victory, the Americans said.

Commodore Macdonough, himself, fired the first gun from the flagship. Death shrieked through the air, ugly and resistless; the ball fairly mowed down the men as it whizzed the entire deck-length of the "Confiance."

The men on the Saratoga shivered as the smoke lifted and they saw the devastation and the gallant enemy advance, without reply. Then at the distance of a quarter of a mile Captain Downie anchored and the other British vessels came to.

The Americans continued to pound away—still the "Confiance" did not respond until secured. Then, with startling suddenness she seemed to point all her guns at the "Saratoga" and become a solid sheet of flame. The air rocked with the blazing of the cannon.

This broadside, from point-blank range, carried destruction to its target. It came terribly, and in turn sang its death-song to the Ameri-cans through the morning air.

When the eddying smoke cleared it seemed to Commodore Mac-donough that he saw half his crew lying on the deck, stunned, wounded or killed by this one discharge—forty was the actual num-ber, out of his two hundred and twelve men. Hammocks were cut to pieces in the netting and bodies cumbered the deck. But presently the "Saratoga" recovered and resumed her animated fire, steady as ever.

Fifteen minutes after the enemy anchored an English vessel was captured, and on Crab Island where there was a hospital and a battery of one gun, the "invalids" took a second.

Sometimes the galleys of the two navies would lie within a boat's hook of each other and the sailors, not liking such close quarters, would rise from the sweeps, ready to spring into the water. It was close and hot—this little naval battle—but gradually, as the guns were injured, the cannonading ceased.

Morgan and Captain Dulaney galloped from place to place for a better view, the old horse prancing at the terrific sound of the firing, never having seemed so full of spirit; constantly he raised his head to sniff the smoke of battle-as if it were a call from his kins-steeds. The clatter of his own hoofs beat loud in his ears; his heart was like to burst with patriotic ardor at the flying flags, the quick orders of the officers, the martial noises, and the sense of peril. He was mad with excitement.

Suddenly from the men on shore burst a cheer, loud and high in exultation; the feeling of pride ran hot in Morgan's veins, he tasted all the sweets of conquest, and raising his head high, added his voice to theirs in a great cry of triumph.

And this was Victory! It was worth—that one moment—his whole long life of hard work and painful partings!

CHAPTER XXI.

DOWN HILL.

For days after the naval battle Morgan seemed rejuvenated, ready to begin life all over; life, with its changes of owners, its partings, its hard work—but withal, its friendships, its moments of supreme joy and exaltation.

It might be well to end the story of old Justin Morgan as he stood there—so fine in his spirit and ambition—watching the fight from the hill commanding the lake; but one or two more incidents remain to be related which will show still greater powers of endurance and patience in his long, hard, but nevertheless, noble life.

On the heels of the American victory came the news that the Dulaneys had been ordered back to West Point, and would not take Morgan with them. It was a bitter parting for the old horse and need not be dwelt upon. All three realized fully, they should never meet again.

* * * *

From Burlington Morgan was sold to Joel Goss and Joseph Rogers, and taken to Claremont, New Hampshire. Here his stable was at the ferry, on the Connecticut River, and the sight of the stream recalled his youth.

He dreamed sweet dreams of colthood; visions of his mother, of Caesar, of Black Baby, came to him and he was content.

But, alas, this pleasant, peaceful life ended full soon, and, in 1816 he was sold to a man by the name of Langmaid, who drove the freight-stage from Windsor to Chelsea, a distance of nearly two hundred miles. Thus the brave old animal, at twenty-seven years of age, was ignominiously thrust into harness company with five other lazy, ill-bred brutes, who dawdled along the road with slack tugs and made the patient Morgan do most of the pulling.

For the first time in his long life the ambitious horse admitted a feeling of discouragement into his heart; he was ill-fed, never rubbed down, and life seemed utterly hopeless.[14]

That was the year men called "Eighteen-hundred-and-starved-to-death," and throughout the entire summer there was not one warm, sunshiny day.

Growing wet with their intolerably toilsome exertions over the slippery, tumbling roads, with the wind howling and the trees bending low about them, the horses would become chilled to the bone, with often nothing but hemlock boughs to eat. They panted and strained as they climbed, and the lumbering stage, with its heavy load of freight, had to be hauled over the tops of the almost perpendicular hills and mountains, at the crack of a long, keen whip in the hands of a merciless driver; every moment they were in danger of crashing over an embankment. It took steady nerve to do this, and poor, proud Morgan, who had never before felt a whip, chafed under the treatment and the remarks of people who had known him in his prime.

He almost fretted himself to death, he was heartsick, and a leaden weariness of battling came over him; he was in a pitiable plight.

That year crops were all killed, famine threatened, and once more Vermont drank the cup of desolation to its dregs. Good church people, with their children starving, cursed their God.

On one occasion the stage passed the farm of a man driven to desperation by the conditions—no crops—no food. He did not hear the stage coming—the horses' feet fell noiselessly on the soundless road, knee-deep—the heavy wheels half hidden—in mud. There he stood, his Bible in his hand, and in a loud voice he poured forth a torrent of threats "to burn the Book if his crops were killed by the threatening frost."

Mother Nature had made her plans, and did not change them for such impious railings.

When the stage passed, a few days later, neighbors' tongues buzzed with Diah Brewster's blasphemy, for he had kept his word!

No one could suggest a punishment to fit the crime, although there were stocks and branding for lesser misdemeanors, such as drunkenness and lying.

Unfortunately, the stage had to go on before the driver found out what decision the Selectmen arrived at as to proper and appropriate penalty.

Soon after this Joseph Rogers chanced to be in Chelsea when the stage coach drew up. Hearing his familiar voice, Morgan—wretchedly miserable and homesick—gave a friendly and anxious whinney. Rogers would never have recognized him otherwise, but as he looked into the horse's kind, gentle face he knew it was his old friend. He started in surprise at the forlorn appearance of the once beautiful horse, now friendless and forgotten.

That evening Morgan was bought back by Joel Goss and Joseph Rogers, who took him again to Claremont, where he soon regained strength and flesh. His coat took on such a gloss that after a while they began to "spruce" him up for the Randolph Fair. And at twenty-eight years of age!

The fair proved to be a very fine one and there were bread-stuffs, pies and quilts of every description, linen and woolen woven by the women, and the men exhibited their fine horses, cows and pigs.

Morgan's stable was as popular as ever and pretty soon the judges gave him a blue ribband, though there were many younger horses in his class who arched their necks and attracted attention.

The chief topic of conversation at the fair was the approaching visit of President James Monroe, who was coming to view the scene of the great naval battle at Burlington. Morgan heard the talk outside his stall.

"They tell me the Morgan goes up to Burlington for the President to ride in the big parade," said a stable boy.

"Yes," some one replied, "Joel Goss wants to sell the horse and thinks with the reputation of having been ridden by a President he'll get a better price!"

"That sounds reasonable—if Morgan was younger."

"Younger? Why, man, this horse'll never grow old! Wait and take a look at him."

The "old" horse was led out, bold and ambitious, his eyes bright, his ears pointing, his spirit fresh as ever! He stepped smartly about, supple and sound as a horse of ten, at the most. It is the spirit that makes the horse and there was a springiness of youth in his gait. Well had he known—this wise animal—that every trait and characteristic he developed in himself would be his gift to posterity! His feeling of responsibility to future generations was great.[15]

A week later the Morgan was led to the Tavern entrance in Burlington. He stepped nobly, and understood all the paces and evolutions of a showy parade-horse.

At the door of the Tavern appeared a man, noticeable for that dignified and courtly bearing that marked the Colonial gentleman. He was attired in a costume of the latest cut—somewhat new to the Vermonters.

He raised his hat and bowed to the right and left as cheer after cheer rose from the people who recognized their President.

Accompanied by General Joseph G. Swift, he started down the steps.

Suddenly over the face of President James Monroe there passed a look of keen interest, followed by one of intense admiration.

He had caught sight of Morgan, and his eye, unerring in its judgment of horseflesh, was arrested at once by his vigorous and fearless style. He turned to a group of officials.

"I see, gentlemen," he said, in a tone of genuine appreciation, "that Vermont can produce a horse worthy of her heroes!"

A moment later and he had thrown his leg over the back of the proudest horse in America!

THE END.

Morgan passed the remainder of his life in the kind care of Mr. Bean, of Chelsea. He died from the effects of a kick from another horse, in 1821, at the advanced age of thirty-two years.

[14] Editor *American Horse Breeder*:—I am an old man, eighty-three, this month, and seeing an article in your last in praise of the Morgan Horse, I want to add a word of gratitude for their noble service done me as a stage-proprietor on the Fourth New Hampshire Townpike; as livery man and farmer.... For endurance, intelligence and as trappy drivers, the Morgans have no equals. To handle six or eight horses on a stage-coach over hills—without accident—looks to me wonderful now, for brakes were not known in those days. I sometimes think it could not have been done without the Morgan horses, for their superior intelligence was often displayed in cases of danger—like running on icy, sidling roads, where every tug was needed, and the horses on the run, to prevent the coach from falling off the bank! I have often done this and seen others do it, and accidents were few. These horses seemed to know what was wanted and understood the danger as well as the driver. It was sometimes no easy matter to carry the mails through blinding sleet and heavy drifts, but I never had a Morgan horse look back to refuse me. They always faced the blast. If a double trip had to be made the *Morgans* always did it and the long-jointed, over-reaching, interfering span of some other breed was kept in the barn.

Yours,

J. C. Cremer, Hanover, N. H.
American Horse Breeder, 1892.

[15] "I see horses every day with, perhaps, a thirty-second part of the blood of Old Justin Morgan, but there it is, still predominating; there is the *Morgan* still to be seen plainly. Every close observer, every discerning judge of horses always admits this tendency of his blood."—From an article by James D. Ladd, *Wallace's Monthly*, July, 1882.

POSTWORD.

The stable of the late George Houstoun Waring, of Savannah, at Annandale Stock Farm, where the first Georgia Morgans were raised, consisted of four Morgans brought from Vermont and New Hampshire. They were, ENTERPRISE, No. 423, chestnut with flaxen mane and tail; PARAGON BLACK HAWK, the handsomest horse I ever saw, black with white star, very showy in tandem; CLIVE, beyond compare in Morgan perfection, for whom, at four years of age Mr. Waring refused $4,000; BAY COMET, perfect in form and disposition, dark with black points. There were fifty mares, nearly all Morgans. The finest of these was ROSALIE MORGAN, from Vermont. She was exhibited many years at the Georgia State Fairs, and at each would take the prizes for the best brood mare, best mare with colt at her side, and best trotting mare. When she appeared in these three classes no other mare stood any chance. Finally she was ruled out. She had nineteen colts, two of which I know sold for $600 each. Rosalie died at thirty-two years of age.

I bought from Mr. Waring a Bay Comet colt, daughter of AMANDA MORGAN, and named her JEANNIE DEAN. Jeannie was like a member of my family for thirty-one years. She was the perfect type in character and form.

FRANK, a grandson of ENTERPRISE, one of the later and best known Morgans was owned and trotted by William Henry Stiles, in 2:18¼; he inherited all the fine traits of "OLD JUSTIN MORGAN."

ANNANDALE had a half-mile track, and every equipment for the care and comfort of this transplanted race.

The farm was situated in Habersham Co., in a luxuriant rolling valley of the beautiful mountainous section of Northeast Georgia; a section almost exclusively occupied by the summer estates of the wealthy rice and cotton planters of the Low Country.

J. W. BRYAN.

DILLON, GEORGIA, September, 1911.